Sargent's face turned purple. "This is my copy desk, and we do things my way," he shouted. He took a deep breath. "You're off the series."

I looked at him without replying. I knew my job was hanging by the most frayed of threads.

He continued bellowing: "And let me warn you — you need to learn how things run in this newsroom. And you need to learn to think with your mouth shut. If you don't, you're not going to last in this business."

I watched him walk out of the newsroom.

"Damn you, bastard," I said, after he was gone. I was trembling. "I'll show you who's off the case."

Sargent and Blazer didn't know me very well. I was as stubborn as they came when I was in a corner. My grandmother, the church, and the public school system had done everything in their power to make me into something I would never be: a quiet, submissive, God-fearing, heterosexual Southern Baptist. You have to possess a strong will to stand up to that onslaught.

Sargent and Blazer were in for the fight of their lives.

Authors Note

This book is a work of fiction. Frontier City, its institutions, and its inhabitants are creations of my imagination. Its newspapers, the *Times* and *Herald,* are not intended to bear any resemblance to any daily newspaper in Oklahoma or elsewhere.

EDITED OUT

1 A CARMEN RAMIREZ MYSTERY

LISA HADDOCK

MYST
HADDO

The Naiad Press, Inc.
1994

Printed in the United States of America on acid-free paper
First Edition

Edited by Katherine V. Forrest
Cover design by Pat Tong and Bonnie Liss
    (Phoenix Graphics)
Typeset by Sandi Stancil

Library of Congress Cataloging-in-Publication Data

Haddock, Lisa, 1960–
    Edited out / by Lisa Haddock.
        p.   cm.
    ISBN 1-56280-077-9
    1. Women journalists—United States—Fiction.   I. Title.
PS3558.A31195E34   1994
813'.54—dc20   93-47338
                                                      CIP

To Lisa Bell,
friend and partner;

and Ena Corinne Foley,
my grandmother,
1908–1983.

Acknowledgements

I am grateful to Lisa Bell and Steven Evan Long for their assistance and suggestions in editing early drafts of this book. I also thank Katherine V. Forrest of the Naiad Press, Inc. for her invaluable editing expertise.

I owe a great debt to the many fine teachers I encountered in the Tulsa public schools and at the University of Tulsa. And finally, I offer love and special thanks to my friend and partner, Lisa Bell, all my relatives — especially my parents and sister — and my friends.

About the Author

Lisa Haddock was born in Tulsa, Oklahoma, in November 1960. She holds a bachelor of arts in mass media news and a master of arts in modern letters, both from the University of Tulsa. Like Carmen Ramirez, she is of Puerto Rican and Irish heritage. A journalist working in New Jersey, she lives with her life partner and two cats.

Suffer little children to come unto me, and forbid them not; for of such is the kingdom of God.

Luke 18:16

CHAPTER 1

Oklahoma, 1985, Late Summer

Midnight. The newsroom was quiet — by newspaper standards. The police radio squawked, three televisions and a radio hummed in the sports department, and, in the distance, members of the cleaning crew chatted boisterously to one another.

Few people were at work in the vast, modern room — decorated in sea-green carpet, cadet blue walls, and dove-gray desks. All the bigwigs, who by day inhabited the glassed-in offices along the walls, and most everybody else had gone home hours ago.

We on the copy desk — the folks who are supposed to catch all the mistakes and write catchy headlines and succinct captions — were marking time until our shift ended by reading unwieldy feature stories for the fat Sunday edition. Two deadlines had passed for that morning's paper; two editions were already being trucked out to our readers.

"Jesus H. Christ," shouted Ralph Sargent, our copy chief, the man with the last say over what made it into the paper. A tough-looking fellow with a white brush-cut and a large belly, Sargent began pounding the keys on his computer as he muttered to himself. One of us was about to get one of his notes, which would highlight the error in the text and add a rebuke, such as: Fix mistakes. Don't add them.

The pounding stopped. Sargent had transmitted the message. I waited a few seconds. No message-pending signal flashed on my screen. I was in the clear. It was somebody else's foul-up.

12:15. Sargent called out: "That's it, folks. I'll be at Bailey's. The first round's on me."

The old warhorse was all smiles again. His face was still slightly flushed, but his round paunch was shaking with laughter as the copy editors bid him good night. Sargent had been at the *Times* since 1950, after World War II duty with the Marines and college on the GI Bill. After several years of reporting, he moved to the copy desk in the late fifties. He became copy chief in 1965 and had been humiliating, harassing, and belittling his underlings ever since. Now he was within a couple of years of retirement.

"When are you going to let me buy you a drink, Carmen?" he called out to me.

I was straightening my desk for the night. I rounded up my note pad, pencils, dictionary, and thesaurus, and tucked them into a desk drawer.

"Live it up," added John Gruber, a fellow copy editor.

"Not tonight, guys," I said, picking up my briefcase.

"Walk you to your car?" John said.

After hesitating, I said: "Okay. Sure."

Frontier City was crime-ridden, and after dark, downtown was among the worst parts of town. Our building was flanked by dark, ominous bars patronized by rough, greasy, long-haired men. John, a pudgy, short, nervous fellow from rural southeastern Missouri, would be of no help should trouble erupt. I regretted letting him tag along, again.

The mid-September night air was still heavy and warm as we approached my car, a new, bottom-of-the-line, navy blue Honda Civic. Its only extras were air conditioning — a necessity for Oklahoma's lengthy, broiling summers — and an AM/FM radio. I could afford the payments only because I rented a garage apartment from my grandmother. Despite the *Times'* sizable circulation of 150,000 daily and 225,000 on Sundays and feeble opposition from an afternoon paper less than half our size, management paid us as if we were working for a weekly paper in the wilds of Idaho.

"I love your car," John said. "When are you going to take me for a ride?"

Why did it always end this way? "Oh, I don't know," I said. "I've got to check on Grandma."

John looked at me with sheepish desire. I started the car, and he stepped onto the curb. I sped away. No more Ms. Nice Guy with John, I decided. I had to make things all-business with him from now on.

The downtown streets were deserted, and within minutes, I was sailing along on the Crosstown Highway, a spur of Interstate 44.

I was born and raised in Frontier City, population 375,000, in the heart of Northeastern Oklahoma. I grew up on land that had once been given forever by the U.S. government to the Creek Nation. Less than a century ago, Frontier City had been Frontier Village: a grubby little trading post town run by whites who peddled inferior goods to the Creeks and to the cowboys who stopped along the banks of the Arkansas River before driving their herds of Texas beef to the railroads up north. The discovery of oil had brought vast wealth and rapid expansion.

These days, the Chamber of Commerce calls Frontier City "America's Hometown" — a brash, new, shining city, filled with friendly people.

The city is carefully partitioned to support that image. The muddy, polluted Arkansas River divides industrial from non-industrial. On the river's west bank, the petroleum refineries pump money into the economy, filth into the river, and a burning, sulfuric stench into the air. Surrounding these reeking industrial giants are blue-collar neighborhoods

4

inhabited by refinery workers and their families. General Boulevard runs through the heart of the city. The farther south you travel from the Boulevard, the richer the neighborhoods become. The farther north, the poorer.

Throughout the city's history, blacks were quite simply not allowed to live, shop, or eat south of the Boulevard. Although the color barrier has broken down somewhat since the late seventies, blacks who have crossed the Boulevard to buy or rent their homes have too often found chilly receptions from their new neighbors.

City government, from the mayor's office to the Sewage Department, favored South over North, and East over West. Good service followed the money. Schools, bridges, roads, and water mains were kept in sparkling condition on the right side of town, while West and North siders coped with decaying schools, gaping potholes, and hemorrhaging water mains.

From the highway, I could see the golden, glowing praying hands atop the Rev. Lovell Taft's thirty-story prayer center. Taft, a Pentecostal tent evangelist and healer, had parlayed his expressive voice and dramatic personality into a worldwide ministry. His sprawling Lovell Taft University and Worldwide Healing Ministry Headquarters dominated fifty acres of prime real estate on Frontier City's posh, lily-white South Side.

Fifteen minutes later, I pulled into my driveway, in the Central part of town. It was a white, solidly blue-collar neighborhood. As usual, the light was burning in the living room of Grandma's home, a small sixty-year-old white frame house with a large screened-in porch. She and my grandfather moved there back in the mid-Thirties. She has been a widow for all of my life.

I let myself in through the front door. My sixty-nine-year-old grandma, Edna Sullivan, sat in her golden, crushed-velvet La-Z-Boy recliner, her steely white hair back in a long braid, her blue eyes trained on *Late Night With David Letterman*. She wore one of her summer cotton nighties and was smoking a small cigar — a habit she hid from the ladies in her Sunday school class at the Fourteenth Street Baptist Church. The television was turned up loud to compensate for the whirring of the attic fan.

"Hi, Grandma," I said, handing her the first edition of the *Times*.

"Thanks," she said, glancing over the front-page headlines. "You write any of these, girlie?"

I pointed to a story on the bottom of the page. GOVERNOR TO MEET WITH JAPANESE DELEGATION.

"I wouldn't trust those rotten little yellow bastards any further than I could throw them." She glanced back at the TV and puffed her cigar. Her foul mouth also was muzzled come Sunday morning.

"I'm hungry, Grandma," I said. "I'm going to scrape myself up a midnight snack."

I headed to the back door. "Lock this behind me," I said.

She waved dismissively. "God protects me," she said. "I feel sorry for the son of a bitch who takes me on."

My apartment was perched over the garage, a few feet behind Grandma's house. I had badgered her for a couple of months before she agreed to let me move in here. She had wanted me to stay with her in the house. She had not rented the apartment out for years. I'd spent a couple of weeks cleaning the place up, sanding, painting, putting up shelves, tearing out the old, rotten carpet, and refinishing the hardwood floor. I paid her two hundred a month in rent. We split the utility bills down the middle; I paid for my own phone.

I scaled the stairs and shoved opened the door. Wiley and Holly — my two cats — ran to my legs as soon as I got in. "Hello, boys," I said.

Wiley — small, shiny, gray, and lithe — replied: "Goow mink mink now." He stretched his front paws, ruffled his fur, and lifted his tail for me.

Holly — a squatty butterscotch tabby — blinked at me. I had originally named him Holiday Inn because he had been a hotel for a parasite convention when I adopted him and Wiley from the city animal shelter, where they had been cellmates. But the name Holly had stuck. When I bent to pick up the mail, Holly licked my hand.

"That's the way to get on my good side," I said. "Now, if only I could get somebody human to do that."

The house was stuffy, so I opened a window and started up the window fan. I leafed through the mail. Jane Swensen's familiar neat printing on a lavender envelope caught my attention. I ripped open the letter.

Dear Carmen:
    I hope all is well with you.

Rita and I have just settled into a new apartment. You would love it. It's right in the middle of the Central West End.

School is as rough as ever, with comps looming this January.

The letter droned on: Rita's lucrative law practice, Rita's work two nights a month at a battered women's shelter; Jane, despite being busy as a PhD candidate in women's literature, was trying to persuade the Womyn's Coffeehouse committee into running alcohol-free, smoke-free events. I skimmed until I got to the last paragraph:

Rita and I hope that someday we will all be friends again and that you will find the healing space within you.

"Bitches," I said, sinking onto the sofa. I crumpled the letter and threw it onto the floor. Sure, we could be friends — like Medea and Jason and his new girlfriend.

Grandma had pronounced me a "hell-bound reprobate" and Jane "a godless, shameless pervert" when I told her I was a lesbian and that we were moving to St. Louis together. Nine months later, Jane told me that she and Rita, her ex-lover, had decided to "share space" and "re-pairbond." However, Jane assured me that I could hang around in her apartment until I could get on my feet. I had a part-time job as clerk at the *St. Louis Morning Record* and couldn't afford to live on my own. Despite the fact that Jane thought my grandmother was full of "negative energy," I quit my job and headed back to Grandma and Frontier City — broke and grief-stricken.

After months of depression verging on coma, I was starting to feel human again. But I still was left with pockets of senseless rage. For instance, anything to do with the St. Louis Cardinals, Rita's beloved team, drove me into a frenzy. The mere sight of Ozzie Smith handspringing across the Astroturf made me want to reach for an AK-47 and launch a one-woman attack on Busch Stadium.

I often wondered why Jane didn't assail Rita as "male-identified" for loving Major League baseball. Maybe it was the fact that Rita — a five-foot-eleven vegetarian fitness fanatic who ran incessantly and who could probably bench-press a truckload of tofu — was unwilling to take shit off anyone.

"Yeah," I said to the crumpled letter on the floor. "Live and let live. Like hell."

I had lost my appetite, so I crawled into bed.

The next night was slow in the newsroom. I had been bored as hell reading about council meetings in nearby small towns, drug arrests in the North Side housing projects, and obituaries.

A *message-pending* signal flashed on my computer screen.

Carmen:
We've got a special project we want you to handle.
See me at the end of the shift.
Sargent

What did it mean? I had been at the paper about eight months — still waiting to graduate from Sargent's boot camp.

All of us plowed through the remaining copy until shortly after midnight, when Sargent made his usual offer of drinks at Bailey's.

I tidied up my desk and then headed toward his desk, at the top inside of a horseshoe of terminals. Copy desks are often arranged this way; so head copy editors are called the "slot men" or "slots" in newspaper lingo. Running a copy desk is often called "working the slot." Those of us who sit outside the horseshoe "work the rim."

Sargent's work area was littered with debris — honey bun and Milky Way wrappers, Styrofoam cups, and paper plates. Sargent continued staring at his screen. He was scanning the sports wire for baseball scores.

"What's up, Ralph?" I said.

"Oh, yes, Carmen, sit down," he said, motioning toward a nearby chair. "You familiar with the Barrett case — that lesbian teacher who murdered the twelve-year-old girl and then killed herself?"

The notorious Barrett case. A mere mention was enough to make any lesbian in a five-hundred-mile radius blush a deep crimson. I was no different. "Well, Ralph, uh, I was in St. Louis when the story broke. My background on the case isn't really that good."

"Well, it's coming up on the two-year anniversary, and special projects is cooking up a series."

"A series — on the killing?" I said.

"The killing, homosexuals in the classroom, the threat they pose, that line of stuff. I want you to

10

work on it. You'll be dealing with Jeff Green. Thinks his copy is pure gold, but, believe me, you'll have to be tough on him. He's a long-winded bastard."

"Who's the assignment editor?"

"Blazer."

Jeff Green and Ron Blazer. It's a wonder they didn't build a new wing just to house their egos. Still in his twenties, Green, a former cop reporter, seemed to have a rocket attached to his career. I couldn't understand how he could give up the gore of police work to cover City Hall and then special assignments. He loved to wolf down drippy barbecued beef sandwiches while bragging about all the sprayed-out brains and ripped-up flesh he had seen at crime scenes. He also liked to bray about laying pipe with a new babe. Blazer, in his forties, had a reputation among copy editors for being hostile and uncommunicative.

And why me on the series? As far as I was aware, no one at the paper knew that I was a lesbian. Frontier City wasn't the kind of place where a queer could flame with impunity. Why Sargent would have chosen me for such an assignment, if, indeed, he had, was puzzling. The copy desk was stratified, and I was clearly on the bottom. Sargent sent me Page One copy rarely. At any other newspaper of our size, I would have been considered too green for the copy desk; I would have been a clerk. But the *Times* was willing to hire inexperienced people on the copy desk. We worked cheap. In fact, I had made a dollar more per hour when I was a clerk in St. Louis.

Byron Kane, Sargent's longtime drinking buddy and fellow veteran of many *Times* battles, was at the top of the heap on the copy desk, the chief's right-hand man. Kane ran the desk on Sargent's nights off. When he wasn't in the slot, he exclusively handled prestige copy — stories running on Page One and the B section front. If the series were considered important, it would be sent to Kane. So either Kane didn't want to handle the series, or it was considered a low priorty.

Gruber, the Missouri boy who would probably pass out (or jerk off) at the word "lesbian"; Max Connor, king of the cute headline (DYKE KILLS TYKE might be his approach); mother-of-two Marian Foster, who probably never heard the word "lesbian"; Pete Simpson, a total lush who was never allowed to edit anything in front of Page A-4 (he probably couldn't even spell "lesbian"); Dave Baker, our baby-faced University of Kansas graduate (he didn't look old enough to shave); and Rhonda Sears, a Lovell Taft alum who no doubt subscribed to the Anita Bryant theory of homosexuality. That left the part-timers, who didn't pull enough hours to handle such a project.

"When do I start?"

"Tomorrow night."

I headed for the door.

"See you at Bailey's?

"I've got to run, Ralph. Thanks anyway," I said, fully intending to head straight home.

On the way down the stairs, I realized I didn't want to go home. I felt my throat tighten. I was lonely, bored, isolated, and tired of the company of crass heterosexuals. I didn't have one real friend in the newsroom, somebody who knew me for who I was.

It was time to be around my own kind. It was true. I needed to get back in circulation. Princess Charming was not going to come riding up on her black Harley and carry me off to her castle.

In Frontier City, that left me with one choice: Crystal's, the only women's bar within ninety miles. I called Grandma from the security guard's station in the lobby. She picked up the phone on the second ring. "Grandma?" I said.

"On your way home, girlie," she said. It was an order, not a question.

It's my life. "No. I'm going out."

She paused. "What are you up to?"

"Nothing," I said. "I just didn't want you to worry."

My heart was pounding as I walked to my car. It had been a long time since I'd been to Crystal's. I tried to be optimistic. *Who knows? I'm not hideous. Maybe I'll meet somebody.*

I hummed "Cabaret" as I drove east.

My heart sank as soon I drove into the parking lot of the rundown little East Side tavern. There were only about ten cars there.

The crowd was sparse in the dark, smoky bar. I scanned the back room. The walls were decorated with black velvet paintings of nude blondes with enormous breasts — the same tacky pictures that were up the last time I was there. A few women were shooting pool. They seemed like serious players, so I decided not to try to chat with them. Johnny Lees "Lookin' for Love" was playing on the jukebox.

The dance floor was empty. A couple at a corner table were kissing so intensely that they seemed on the verge of having sex. *Lord. Everybody's got a pal but me.*

I looked at my watch. 12:30. If the place wasn't hopping by then, it wasn't going to be. I sat at the bar, which was long and black. The only other patron there was a middle-aged woman with unkempt, shoulder-length dyed red hair. Wearing a shabby denim workshirt and jeans, she had a bottle of Jack Daniels beside her and seemed intent on drinking herself into the International Dipsomaniac Hall of Fame.

I looked away. Crystal, herself, was presiding. A wide, strong woman with an impressive white crew cut, she was a regal presence among the bottles of booze, the mirrored walls, and the twinkling Christmas lights.

"I'll have to see some ID, kiddo," she said. Her accent was pure West Texas: the distinctly Southwestern sound of a permanent head cold.

I handed her my driver's license with a trembling hand. The photo made me look like a half-wit.

"Take it easy. I ain't a-gonna bite you," she said with a laugh. She peered at the license through her wire-rimmed half-glasses, which she wore on a cord around her neck. Hmm, twenty-four, well that makes you old enough in my book. What'll it be?"

"What kind of beer do you have?" I said weakly.

Crystal began her list: Bud and Bud Light on tap; in bottles, Michelob, Michelob Light, Lowenbrau, Heineken, Foster's.

"Foster's," I said. Not my favorite Bass Ale, but it

would do in a pinch. And this was a pinch. I desperately needed something to boost my spirits.

"Not much of a crowd tonight, huh?"

"Nope. 'Fraid not," Crystal said. She resumed wiping the bar.

I got up and walked over to the jukebox. Most of the songs had changed since my last visit, when I first returned to Frontier City over a year ago, but the flavor was the same. One-third country, one-third top forty, and the rest sleazy dance mixes from the men's bars.

Jane. No matter how much I tried to hate her, ignore her, forget her, I couldn't keep her out of my thoughts. I had met her on Halloween weekend in 1982 during a camping trip sponsored by the Progressive Students Coalition. I was a twenty-one-year-old senior in the Frontier City University journalism program. Despite my success in academic matters (I was an A student and editor of the campus newspaper) I was living in terror. I knew I was a lesbian, but I was scared to death to tell anybody else, let alone act on my feelings. Deep in the woods next to the gray-green Grand River, I had spotted Jane, a twenty-six-year-old graduate student in the women's literature program at FCU, and the most obvious lesbian I had ever seen. She was a short, sturdy woman, clad in baggy khakis and a big wool sweater, with close-cropped sandy brown hair and luminous blue eyes. I fell in love instantly. For the rest of the weekend, I followed her everywhere. She was everything I wanted to be — strong, confident, voluble, well-read, radical, and openly lesbian. Jane spouted politics all weekend as I soaked up her every word.

She and I had come to Crystal's soon after we became lovers. Our trip to the bar had been disastrous. Jane didn't drink — alcohol is a poison, she always told me — and I ended up having a few too many beers and pleading with Jane to get on the dance floor with me. She had said she couldn't dance in an environment polluted by heterosexist music, so we ended up going home early.

Jane. I was alone in this dingy bar with no one to talk to. Jane, who was playing house with Rita in St. Louis, was still haunting my memories. And my life still sucked.

I slipped a dollar in Crystal's tip jar and headed for the door.

CHAPTER 2

The next day, Grandma was spoiling for a fight. She insisted on weeding the flower bed right underneath my apartment, and every so often she would glower up toward my windows, a ploy to catch my eye. I refused to be baited. I spent the morning and early afternoon in a cleaning frenzy — washing dishes, dusting, sweeping, and scrubbing the bathroom.

Around two, I showered for work. I wanted to get in early so I could read the *Times'* previous stories about the Barrett case. I pulled on some Levis, a blue button-down oxford shirt, and a pair of black cloth Converse high-tops. The dress code on the night shift was very relaxed. Only Sargent clung to the formality of a dark suit, white shirt, and tie. I always brought along a sweater because the air conditioning made the newsroom feel like a meat locker.

I combed my hair back. I was too cheap to run the air conditioner in my apartment except on the hottest of days, so blow-drying would be madness. I kept my thick black hair short, so there was little need to fuss, except for a little hair spray.

By this time, the mid-afternoon heat had driven Grandma back to the house, so I made a run for my car. I had just opened the door when Grandma, frantically wiping her hands on her apron, came steaming toward me.

"Where were you, girlie?"

I won't let her get to me. "We're not going to have this discussion. I am an adult."

"A little ways back you didn't seem so high and mighty. You were blubbering and bawling like a three-year-old over that *friend* of yours."

The words stung. The old girl knew how to hit where it hurt.

I cleared my throat. "Grandma, if you're going to give me hell every time I go out, then I'll move out as soon as possible."

She paused. "Are you getting in with those damn perverts again?"

"Give me a break," I said.

"I should have never let you stop going to church."

I started the car and backed out of the driveway. *Let her be as mad as she wants.*

I got to work an hour early, but the street parking spaces around the *Times* building were jammed. I ended up parking in a lot, which I hated to do. I put enough money in the slot for three hours. I could move the car to street parking on my break. I could park for free after six.

During the day, the air was filled with noise as reporters badgered their sources over the phone and shouted at one another and their editors. At night, a no-nonsense atmosphere took over, as copy editors sifted through hundreds of green characters glowing on black screens. We searched for misspelled words, factual errors, and just plain bad writing.

I logged onto a computer usually used by Dan Johnson, the outdoor writer. He was probably out reeling in some trophy-size bass or blasting away at a ten-point buck. His cubicle was plastered with pictures of animals he had just "harvested."

By using any terminal in the newsroom, it was possible to log onto the newspaper's library database. By typing a few simple commands, users could search for stories by name, word, phrase, dateline, headline, date, and author.

Ron Blazer — then a senior investigative writer — had been the original reporter on the Barrett story. His writing was vivid. Clearly, he relished his work.

The victim had been twelve-year-old Rebecca Metcalf, daughter of the Rev. Bobby Ray Metcalf, pastor of the sprawling Southside Tabernacle of Hope church and faculty member and trustee at Lovell Taft University. Many observers believed Metcalf was being groomed to take over Taft's ministry; Taft and his wife, Sarah Mae, had no children of their own. Rebecca had been found in the home of Diane Barrett, forty-two, her sixth-grade teacher. Little Rebecca had not died easily. The autopsy showed her face and arms were bruised and lacerated, indicating she had struggled with her killer. The cause of death was a massive blow to the head. Hair and blood at the crime scene showed that she had fallen against the coffee table in Barrett's living room. More ghastly still, the prepubescent youngster's genital area showed signs of violation.

Barrett, a teacher at Washington Elementary School for sixteen years, had graduated with a degree in elementary education from Frontier City University. In the early morning after the killing, Barrett — drunk and nearly incoherent — had called police at 2:35 a.m. to report the slaying. Rebecca had already been dead several hours when police arrived. The only blood found on Barrett had been on her white tennis shoes and on the knees of her jeans. Police were later to conclude that Barrett destroyed the clothes she had worn during the murder. Overcome with remorse, she had drunk heavily for the next several hours after the murder and then decided to call police early that morning.

Days after the crime, Blazer's profile of Barrett was published, cataloguing Diane's history of lesbian attachments and heavy drinking.

A week after the slaying, Barrett, who had been questioned extensively by the police but not charged, committed suicide by taking a massive dose of Valium in combination with alcohol, choking to death on her own vomit, according to the coroner's report. Barrett had not left a suicide note.

Soon thereafter, a grand jury was convened, which concluded that Diane was indeed the culprit. The case was closed.

With time to kill before my shift, I headed to the library for a look at the faces that went with the facts. In addition to picture files, the room housed reference works and microfilm copies of the *Times*. As I rounded the corner, I nearly fell over to avoid slamming into another body. I looked down. Photos of Elvis lay scattered all over the floor.

"That's just the sort of day it's been," said the woman, who was carrying an empty manila folder marked ELVIS PRESLEY.

"I'm so sorry," I said. "Really, I can't believe I did this."

"That's okay." She offered a forgiving smile.

She was college age. She had beautiful green eyes, short blonde hair, and a deep tan. She wore a light blue cotton sweater and light gray dress slacks. A little taller than me, about five-foot-eight, she had the look of an athlete, perhaps a tennis player. I sensed that I had stared a little too long, so I crouched down and began picking up the pictures. She squatted beside me, and I busied myself to avoid looking at her at such close range. After we had finished, she stood up and stuck out her hand to help me up. "Julia Nichols, library clerk," she said.

I grasped her hand. "Carmen Ramirez, news copy editor," I said, getting to my feet.

"Oh, you're a real person?" she said.

"Excuse me?" I said.

"Well, I'm just a lowly clerk. Just a part-timer at that. But you're an editor."

"Oh, that kind of real person. When did you start here?" I said.

"Last week," Julia said. "I'm here for the semester on an internship. I go to FCU. Well, I have to run. The lifestyle editor is calling. She was in a big hurry for these pictures."

"Sorry I held you up."

She dashed off.

Using the automated filing system, I quickly tracked down picture files on Diane Barrett, twelve-year-old Rebecca, and her father.

Barrett's college portraits showed a sincere-looking woman with dark eyes, long, dark hair, and no smile. Her face had been pretty back then, in a subdued, sad way. Twenty years and a murder investigation had ravaged her appearance. A *Times* photographer had captured a shot of Barrett being escorted into the downtown police station by two burly male officers. Barrett's face looked puffy, and her dark eyes revealed an unspeakable sadness. The last shot was of Barrett's sheet-covered corpse being wheeled by ambulance workers out of her small white brick home in Central Frontier City.

Rebecca's file contained several school pictures, including her sixth-grade portrait. A pleasant-looking girl on the verge of puberty, Rebecca had straight, long sandy hair, parted down the middle. Her lips were compressed into a neat, toothless, grownup smile. Her eyes, a shiny blue, looked a little impish. And there was the obligatory shot of her dead body being wheeled out of Barrett's house on a gurney as police officers swarmed in the background.

The shots of the father were varied. Professional portraits showed an earnest man with large blue eyes and dark, straight graying hair swept back in a pompadour. Another shot showed him in action on the podium, his arms stretched out in a crucifixion pose, his face contorted in anguish. Yet another photo — taken as he and his other daughter, Rachel, then sixteen, according to the caption, were going into the funeral — was arresting. Metcalf and his surviving daughter looked like wax figures, their expressions devoid of life as they walked into the chapel at Lovell Taft University, his arm wrapped tightly around her waist, as if he were holding her up.

I returned to the shots of Barrett. This woman appeared joyless even in her college days. What in the world could have made her so sad back then? In the shot of her with the officers, she looked like a cornered rabbit, anything but a murderer, especially the murderer of a child. What could have made her do such a thing? It didn't add up.

Ten to four, time to get to work. I shoved the pictures back into their folders.

Just then, Julia returned. "Can I help you find anything?"

"No, thanks. I'm almost finished here."

"The lifestyle editor took forever to make up her mind which picture she wanted. Then she wanted me to run the picture down to engraving for her. They wanted to use Elvis in color."

"That's okay. Really. I found everything I needed."

"You're sure?"

"Yeah. I'm fine. Thanks."

I waved at Julia and headed for the newsroom.

That night, I handled little work on the Barrett case. I proofread a map of the crime scene, which showed the position of Rebecca's body in the overall layout of Barrett's house. I also read a chronology of Rebecca's last hours. She had shown up at school that day on time at 8:30 a.m., had left school on foot at 3:00 p.m., and arrived home some five minutes later. She had then had a snack with her father. She was supposed to show up at LTU's music building for piano lessons at 4:00 p.m. but never made it. At 2:35 a.m., Diane Barrett called the police to report the discovery of Rebecca's body.

Suddenly it occurred to me that there was no mother in the Metcalf household. Clearly, someone had given birth to these girls. I had to find out who and where she was.

I fixed a couple of typos and then switched to working for the next day's paper. Shortly after midnight, Sargent released us.

As I pulled into my driveway, I saw that the light in Grandma's living room was off. She must have been very upset; Grandma did not give up her late-night TV pleasures lightly. I checked her bedroom window. Sure enough, she was watching Letterman on her black-and-white.

I climbed the stairs to my apartment. The cats were especially glad to see me. Wiley mewed and purred loudly, while Holly sniffed and rubbed at my ankles.

A message waited on my answering machine.

"Carmen, this is your father," announced Raúl Ramirez in his silvery Puerto Rican accent. "Please call me. It is eleven p.m., your time. I will be up late tonight."

My father and I weren't exactly close. My parents had moved from Oklahoma to New York City soon after I was born so that my father, who worked at the time as an accountant for an oil company, could work for a travel agency launched by one of his brothers, Enrique. Shortly before my first birthday, my mother, Anne, was killed in a traffic accident, and my father sent me back to live with Grandma Sullivan. I hadn't seen him all that often when I was growing up, although he called frequently and sent gifts. It hadn't made for a warm relationship.

I dialed Raúl.

"Did I wake you up?" I said.

"No. No. I was just watching the television."

"Well, what's up?"

"How are you?" he said.

"Fine. You?"

"The city is full of criminals and filthy people. But business is good. Your uncle and I are prospering."

"Glad to hear it," I said.

"How is your grandmother?"

I was the only reason the two of them maintained civil-yet-chilly ties. Grandma had despised Raúl since he and my mother first started dating. The idea of her fair, red-headed daughter dating a swarthy Puerto Rican was disgusting to her. She was sure Raúl had a wife and twelve children back on the island and was only using my mother in some ploy to improve his bloodline. Ever the gentleman, Raúl never spoke ill of Grandma although I guessed that he quietly resented her.

"Oh, she's fine. Feisty and mean."

"Do you need anything? Any money?"

I looked around my apartment. My sofa and coffee table were from a thrift store. My pots and dishes were Grandma's castoffs and K-mart specials.

"No. I'm doing okay."

"Do you have yourself a young man yet?"

I took a breath. He would never understand. "No. And don't count on one, either."

"I'm sorry to hear that," he said lightly. "I'm looking forward to being a grandpa."

"Why don't you get yourself a young woman?" I said.

"I have no desire to remarry. Your Tia Teresa takes good care of me."

Lucky Aunt Teresa. Uncle Enrique's wife must be at the stove or the washing machine twenty-four hours a day.

He plodded on: "You sure you don't need anything?"

"Absolutely. But thanks for asking."

"In that case, I will go. God bless you," he said. We hung up.

I took a deep breath. I was depressed.

* * * * *

After a restless night, I awoke at 10:30 and spent the morning scanning the classified ads for a new place to live. I didn't relish the task. I had just gotten settled, and Grandma, despite all her flaws, was the only real family that I had. The late summer heat would make the move harder. And my income was skimpy. I would have to live conservatively so that I could round up enough cash for security deposits. I found about fifteen suitable places in the ads and made note of the addresses and phone numbers.

Around 11:30, Grandma came out of her house and headed for her giant green Ford LTD. She must have been going shopping. Usually, she offered to pick up items for me. But I guess she was too peeved to ask. She was an expert at this freeze-out treatment.

After making a few calls about the apartments — a few turned out to be promising — I put on a Rolling Stones hits tape and threw together some tomatoes, peppers, zucchini, lettuce, and onions from the garden for a salad. I wondered whether Grandma would deny me picking rights in the family patch. I had helped plant that stuff, I shared watering and weeding chores with the old bat, but she might not want to share her produce with a pervert.

My life was beginning to suck like a Hoover again. Too bad Grandma had raised me a Baptist. I felt like going right to a convent. I wouldn't have to worry about where I would live, how I would pay the rent, what to wear, what to eat. Hell, all I'd have to do is hang out with a bunch of women, pray, chant, and wear black. A life I could handle.

After lunch and a long bath, I discovered a couple of bags of groceries at the foot of the stairs leading to my apartment. A note was taped to one of the bags.

Carmen:
You owe me $32.50. I picked up your usual items.
Grandma

Well, at least the old bird didn't want to starve me out. I put away the groceries and headed over to her house. As I walked in the back door, I could see her watching a soap opera.

"Grandma, I'm leaving the money in the kitchen," I called out. "Thanks."

She looked up from the TV and waved dismissively.

So, we were going to play it that way. She was going to keep drawing me in so she could snub me. It was hard to believe that she was nearly seventy years old. She was acting like a fourth-grader. I walked out.

I put on some vintage Peggy Lee as I pondered what I would wear to work. Around the house during the summer, I wore cutoffs and T-shirts. Grandma was horrified that I didn't shave my legs anymore. I picked out a red polo shirt and some roomy khaki slacks. I hated feeling bound up.

* * * * *

The blazing afternoon Oklahoma sun bouncing off the white walls and chrome fixtures made the Metro Coffee shop unbearably bright. So I left on my black Rayban Wayfarer sunglasses as I walked in. The smell of delicious, freshly roasted coffee more than made up for the glare. I ordered an iced coffee and took a corner table so I could study the businessmen and winos wandering around Downtown.

"Hey, what's with the shades?"

Julia Nichols, the library clerk, was standing behind me. She was dressed in white slacks and a loose green shirt.

"Oh, hi," I said. "The light, I mean, don't you think it's a little bright in here?" I put my sunglasses on the table.

"I guess so. I thought maybe you were a movie star trying to avoid the public," Julia said. "Mind if I join you?"

"Not at all," I said. The day was looking better already.

"The computers are down," Julia said, scooting her chair up to the table. "My boss sent us all out for walks."

I tried not to notice how the green in her shirt and the warm light brought out the color of her eyes. I also tried not to notice her long, deeply tanned arms. "So what are you drinking?"

"Orange pekoe-herbal blend." She tilted her head and smiled. A nice smile it was too.

"Sounds good," I said. I cleared my throat. "Nothing like iced tea on a hot day." *Boy, I bet that impressed her.*

"So, Carmen, tell me something."

What could she be after? *Carmen are you a lesbian?* Nah. That couldn't be it. "Sure, what?" I said in feigned nonchalance.

"Is it possible to be an editor and a nice person at the same time?"

I laughed, with relief. "That's certainly a loaded question."

"Well, I have just noticed that most of the editors at the *Times* seem to have huge sticks implanted up their backsides, if you know what I mean."

She was smiling that smile — broad, honest, open, welcoming. Her teeth were perfectly formed and flawlessly white. Didn't she ever turn it off? I chuckled nervously. Why did I always have this problem with attractive women? Because I'd been alone too long. At this point, I would have flirted with Godzilla.

I launched into a speech: "There are a lot of unpleasant people at this paper, but then again, I think a lot of newspaper types are unpleasant. I used to be a news clerk at the *St. Louis Morning Record*. There were more than a few nasty people at that paper. Plus, people tend to take their frustrations out on clerks. At least they did on me."

"So I have more abuse to look forward to?"

"Not from me," I said, too earnestly. I regrouped. "I mean, my memory of clerkdom is still too clear. Typing in temperatures, lake and river levels, obituaries, wedding stories. I did it all. And I didn't like any of it. Besides, I have my own cross to bear with Sargent." That was it: Bore her to death and make myself sound like a martyr at the same time.

Julia laughed. It was a charming laugh, too. I was too lonely to be around such lovely company.

"What's he like to work for?" she said.

"He's a regular Attila the Slot — Scourge of the Copy Desk. He's an old Marine and he puts the new people through boot camp until he gets some new meat to chew on. Unfortunately, I was the last person hired."

"Are you scared of him?"

"Oh, sure, sometimes. But mostly I just get angry. A few times, I was so pissed off that I went to the ladies room to kick one of the stalls or beat up the towel dispenser. I just try to tell myself it's not personal. He treats everybody like dirt at one time or another. Besides, I need a job." Swell. Now I'd made myself sound like a broke masochistic-psycho-loser.

Julia nodded. "Well, I'd better go," she said. "My boss is going to turn into Attila the Librarian if I don't get back soon. He said take a walk, not a twelve-mile hike."

"See you later. Thanks for dropping by. I enjoyed chatting with you." My eyes lingered on her as she walked away. She was tall, attractive, sweet, and she had a shapely bottom to boot. She had a sense of humor and enjoyed laughing. Maybe she liked me, a little. I smiled and began humming "Maria" from *West Side Story*.

A few minutes later, I was back in the newsroom. I searched the database for Mrs. Metcalf, but came up empty. Whoever she was, she did not appear anywhere in our system, which went back two years. I would have to dig through the microfilm archives, and I didn't have time today. Maybe Julia could help. I smiled at the thought.

I logged on to discover a lengthy profile of Diane Barrett. The headline had already been written: A MONSTER IN DISGUISE.

I immediately sent Sargent a note.

Ralph:
Blazer indicates that he wants to use headline describing Barrett as "A Monster in Disguise." I feel this is unnecessary and inflammatory and makes this paper look like the *National Enquirer*. This woman was never convicted of molesting and murdering Rebecca Metcalf. What should I do?

Sargent's reply came quickly.

Carmen:
Leave suggested headline in place. Atop the file, write a note detailing your objections. I will look at it later.
Sargent

I proceeded with the story:

By JEFFREY GREEN
Of The Frontier City Times
To her colleagues, Diane Barrett appeared to be a dedicated teacher. But beneath the facade was a

heavy drinker and child molester who might have abused scores of children.

Barrett, 42, was the prime suspect in the Oct. 17, 1983 sexual molestation and murder of Rebecca Metcalf, her 12-year-old sixth-grade student at Washington Elementary School, on Frontier City's South Side. The teacher committed suicide by a drug overdose shortly after the murder.

Investigators, concluding that Barrett had molested Rebecca and then killed her because the girl had threatened to reveal the abuse to authorities, closed the case.

Rebecca was the daughter of a prominent local minister, the Rev. Bobby Ray Metcalf, pastor of the Southside Tabernacle of Hope, and trustee and faculty member at Lovell Taft University.

Dr. Myra Hawkins, principal of Washington School, described the sixth-grade teacher: "She was one of the most dedicated teachers I have ever worked with. She would put in long hours before and after school. She was always there for the children. I am shocked about the revelations. I still can't take it in."

Ruby Weller, a fifth-grade teacher at Washington School, said: "I worked closely with Diane because a lot of my former students wound up in her class. She seemed to be a very good teacher. In fact, many of my former students used to come back and chat with me about how much they liked her class."

But, according to reports obtained from the police, courts, and the Frontier City Public Schools Administration Center, Barrett had a history of excessive drinking. Court records show that on May

5, 1978, Frontier City police arrested Barrett for driving while intoxicated. Barrett pleaded guilty, paid a fine of $500, and lost her driver's license for three months.

According to a personnel file obtained from the Administration Center, Barrett had been officially warned that any further alcohol-related incidents would lead to the loss of her job.

Psychology professors agreed that it is not unusual for child molesters to drink heavily.

According to Dr. Lawrence Baker of Frontier City University: "Pedophiles are committing socially unacceptable acts. Alcohol and other drugs help quiet the voices of disapproval."

Dr. Harold Simms of Lovell Taft University agrees: "Very commonly, alcohol and drugs accompany this sort of aberrant behavior. Substance abuse certainly doesn't cause the behavior, but it does suppress inhibitions and allow these desires to surface."

But Hawkins did not see the DWI arrest as part of a pattern. Said the principal: "I was aware of Diane's arrest. I thought it was an isolated case of bad judgment on her part."

Another established pattern in Barrett's life was her lesbianism. According to a source who has requested anonymity, Barrett had been a practicing homosexual since her days at Frontier City University.

A former resident of the dormitory where Barrett had lived during her college days said that the future teacher's homosexuality was obvious.

"Everybody knew about Diane," the former resident said. "She lived in a single room and had this same girl stay overnight a lot. We all avoided her [Diane] in the showers."

What was obvious about Barrett during her years at FCU became a well-kept secret later at Washington School.

"I regard my teachers as professionals," said Hawkins. "I never suspected anything about her personal life. There was never any indication that Diane was a lesbian. I didn't pry into her personal life because I didn't see any need."

Weller commented: "I used to offer to fix her up with men, but she never seemed interested. She told me she was seeing someone. I took her at her word."

But Buddy Jefferson, a janitor at Washington School, suspected something was not quite right with the teacher. "She didn't seem to have much use for men. I just picked up a certain feeling about her," he said.

Chances are, Rebecca Metcalf was not Barrett's only victim, the experts agree.

Said Baker: "It is very unusual for a sexual offense to be an isolated event. You have to understand, this is a habitual type of behavior. Usually the offender was abused himself or herself in childhood. When she or he — and most commonly it is a he — starts repeating the pattern of abuse against others, the behavior quickly becomes an addiction. By the time the typical offender is apprehended, he may have abused a great many children.

But how was Barrett able to fool her colleagues?

Said Baker of FCU: "It is not unusual for pedophiles to be respectable members of the community. The stereotype of the old man in the dirty raincoat luring kids into the bushes with candy is simply not always the case. Often pedophiles are teachers, ministers, scoutmasters, priests, choirmasters. Their positions of power and influence shield them from suspicion and allow them to continue their abusive behavior."

And so we are left to wonder: Just how many children did Diane Barrett abuse? It's a question that may never be answered.

My pulse was racing. There was something wrong here, something unfair. I began another note to Sargent.

Ralph:

It seems to me that we're drawing a lot of conclusions based on very little evidence.

We're calling her a heavy drinker based on one incident of drunken driving. And even if she was a heavy drinker, the expert in the story said alcohol doesn't turn somebody into a child molester — it can lower the inhibitions to commit the behavior. We're calling her a lesbian because one woman says that others avoided her in the shower and because a janitor at the school had a funny feeling about her. We're accusing her of molesting any number of children when it's never been proven in court that she molested Rebecca Metcalf. And no other children have come forward to accuse her.

I'm not saying she's innocent, but she was

never proven guilty in a court of law. And by using "monster" in the headline, we are labeling her as wicked, depraved, evil. By implication, we are accusing her colleagues at the school of failing to recognize her as a monster. We should rethink this coverage. It is sensationalistic and possibly inaccurate.

I shipped the story back to Sargent. I didn't know what he would do about the note, or me for that matter.

For the rest of the shift, I edited stories for the next morning's paper. I received no reply from Sargent about the Barrett case, although he berated me twice — over a comma error I had overlooked and for using the word host as a verb. Shortly after midnight, he released us. I was walking out when he offered drinks at Bailey's. As usual, I declined.

CHAPTER 3

Back home, the siege was still on. Grandma was holed up in her bedroom and accepting no late-night visitors, except for her favorite beau, David Letterman.

"The old bat," I said. "Well, she can just rot in there."

I mounted the stairs and received warm greetings from my cats. Wiley, as usual, was vocal in his approval of me, while Holly silently rubbed against me. The living room was in disarray, and Holly and

Wiley looked pleased with their mischief: They had scattered on the floor all of the magazines I had carefully stacked on the coffee table earlier in the day.

"You guys," I said. I checked the mail: nothing personal, just bills and the usual junk. The bills reminded me it would be hard to manage in a more expensive apartment.

I straightened up the mess and then fetched myself a Bass Ale. Hard work deserved a reward, as far as I was concerned.

I settled down on the couch, and Julia drifted into my mind. She was leaning toward me with her head slightly tilted. She was eager to speak with me. She had walked over on her own. Her green eyes were shining. And her lips were smiling in a coy, seductive way. She made a lot of eye contact. She was telling me something, hinting she was gay. *You're out of your mind, Carmen. Seek professional help immediately.*

I flipped my phone book to the D's. I wanted to call up my friend Charles. Charles Dennis and I had been pals since our days as freshmen at FCU. In fact, we had gone through freshman orientation together. Now he was a doctoral candidate in literature at California-Berkeley. I was sure he would have a date. He was a former high school athlete — a member of the varsity swim team — with a mixture of Cherokee and French ancestry: six-foot-four and swarthy, with reddish brown hair and blue-green eyes. Perhaps I could catch him before he went out. Charles picked up on the third ring.

"Carmen. How lovely to hear from you."

"I know you're probably getting ready for a date, but I really needed to talk."

Charles paused dramatically. "No such luck for me. I've been going steady lately. But my beau does quite a bit of traveling, so I'm afraid, for tonight, I'm holing up with some books. My January comp is looming."

"Who is this guy?"

"You're going to laugh, but he's an honest-to-God traveling salesman. He works for a computer company and travels around peddling his wares. His name is Roger."

"I'm happy for you. I hope it works out." Charles fell deeply in love about every ten minutes.

"So what's the trouble? Everything okay with the boss?"

"I'm still his goat, but I'm holding up okay. It's something else. I'm smitten."

"You're not still mooning over the Dreadful Bitch, are you?"

When Charles didn't like someone, he stopped calling him or her by name. Therefore, Jane had become the "Dreadful Bitch."

"No, no. It's somebody new."

"Thank God for that. I trust you are disassembling the shrine."

"That's enough, Charles. Love takes time to get over. You should know that. And besides, you never liked Jane."

"Nonsense. I just adore humorless, self-righteous people who attack everything I do, say, eat, and drink. And besides, she treated you so well."

"She had her good points," I said.

"Well, thank God I never saw them," he said. "So who's the new flame?"

"Her name is Julia. She's a blonde, Charles. With green eyes. She works at the paper."

"So what's the problem?"

"I'm thinking about her a lot. I'm starting to feel things for her."

"Okay, hold on here. Is she a lesbian?"

"I have no idea."

"Oh my God," Charles said. "Just what you need. Pining for the Dreadful Bitch for twelve million years wasn't bad enough. Now you've got the hots for some straight girl."

"It's not the hots. And I don't know that she's straight."

"Oh, honey, it's always the hots. And you need to watch out for yourself."

"I know. I know. I'm just lonely. And Julia seems so nice. She's so pretty."

"So's Stevie Nicks, dear, but you can't have her, either."

"I'm thinking maybe I'll ask her out."

"Stevie?"

"No. Julia."

"Just take it slow, Carmen," he said. "Even if she has sex with you, that doesn't mean she cares anything about you or even that she's a lesbian. A lot of these straight people just want the obligatory gay experience. It's kind of like eating snails. They just want to be able to say they tried it."

"Who's talking about having sex? I haven't even gone out on a date with her. I haven't gone out on a date in forever."

I hadn't dated for a while with good reason.

When I first got back to Frontier City, I'd desperately tried to meet women. I had to be with someone, *anyone* to try to fill the aching hole Jane left in my heart.

The results were disastrous. I suffered countless rejections at local lesbian gatherings and at Crystal's. The women I was chasing sensed that all was not right with me in the mental health department. Who could blame them? I was sleeping fourteen hours a day. During my waking hours, I was working as a file clerk at a clinic, writing masochistic letters to Jane, and acting like a zombie. In the midst of all this psychodrama, I decided to stop trying to date until I could behave like a human being.

"I don't even think I know what to do anymore," I said.

"Oh, don't be silly. Something always comes to mind."

"Please. I'm not talking about sex," I said. "What am I going to do about Julia?"

"All right. Listen to me," he said. "Don't start buying her flowers, don't be the first to say I love you, don't be the first to suggest commitment, and for God's sake, don't pick out rings yet."

"Charles," I said, "have you and Roger picked out rings yet?"

"To tell you the truth, dear, I've had my eye on a pair of simple gold bands."

"And how long have you been going out?"

"Three weeks."

"Three weeks?"

"Just shut up, Carmen. This time it's different. It's fate. We have chemistry. It's like Catherine and Heathcliff."

"For your sake, I hope so."

"Me too."

"I'm dirt poor. I can't afford to talk anymore. Take care of yourself. You are practicing safe sex, aren't you?" I couldn't help nagging him about it.

"Yes, Mother."

"I worry about you."

"I know, sweetie. I appreciate it, too."

"Thanks, Charles. And you keep me posted on Roger."

We hung up. Picking out rings after three weeks? Charles was maturing.

Saturday was my last workday of the week. Ron Blazer worked Monday through Friday, so he hadn't had a chance to review my objections to Green's profile of Barrett. But I wasn't expecting him to be receptive.

Saturdays were easy. The copy desk got in at three. Deadlines were earlier because of the size of the Sunday paper. Most of the sections were printed in advance. Still, the staff had to put out a large number of news pages. Sargent worked Tuesday through Saturday as well, and he was always eager to get an early start on his drinking. At 10:00 p.m., he turned us loose.

Gruber, the lonesome Missouri boy, approached me as I was straightening my desk. "How is our lovely *señorita* tonight?"

The smell of his new cologne sickened me almost as much as did his attempt at Spanish. I had studied Spanish in high school and college and had picked up a few words from my father. But certain people expected me to be able to rattle off the language like a native simply because my name was Carmen Ramirez.

"John," I said in exasperation, "I was born and raised in Oklahoma. English is my native language."

Gruber looked wounded. Maybe he was just trying to be sophisticated. "I'm sorry, Carmen." He seemed sincere.

"It's okay. I've just had to put up with cracks all my life because of my name."

"Why don't you let me make it up to you? How about a drink somewhere?"

"No, John, really I can't."

Tears actually welled up in his large brown eyes. "It's all right. I'm used to rejection," he said.

"You have to understand," I said, "I never go out with co-workers. I try to keep things strictly business."

"I understand. A pretty lady like yourself probably has lots of offers."

"John, you need to broaden your horizons. Join a club. Meet somebody else. You're barking up the wrong tree." Would he get it?

He stared at me. "Couldn't we just be friends?"

I wanted to scream, but instead I took a deep breath. "All right. Just don't push so hard."

"I understand. No pushing from this fellow."

I nearly laughed. I was sure lots of straight women would welcome his ardor.

Gruber followed me down the dark, paneled hall to the elevator. I didn't relish the thought of being trapped in a little box with him, so I headed for the stairs. He followed me like a Labrador puppy. "So, how is it going with that series on the queer teacher? I've been reading it over your shoulder."

"I beg your pardon." This guy was begging to be smacked in the mouth.

"I hope you don't mind. I was just interested in the story. I haven't been fooling with your work."

"I don't care what you read. I object to your use of the word queer."

Gruber looked wounded again. "Geez. A fellow can't say anything right around you."

"John, you just happen to be hitting pretty close to home this evening."

A look of sheer bewilderment swept over his face. We proceeded silently to the lobby.

"Walk you to your car?"

"I'll go it alone this evening."

"Whatever you say, Carmen," Gruber said. "The lady is always right."

I left him standing in front of the building.

I bypassed checking on Grandma. She usually turned in early on Saturday night because she spent most of Sunday at church — where she had sung alto in the choir for forty years, been a member of the Ladies Mission Society, and headed up nearly every committee and bean dinner she could stick her nose into. Since I had been back in town, Grandma had resumed badgering me to return to church. I wouldn't budge.

Since childhood, I had had a stormy relationship with the Baptist Church. It's swallow-it-all-or-roast-in-hell fundamentalism had always set my young mind searching for thorny biblical contradictions to bring up for discussion in Sunday school. Some of my teachers aged visibly when I was under their care. "The Bible is like a sweater," Carmen, they used to say. "If you keep picking at it, it will unravel. You have to accept it all — cover to cover." By the time I reached high school, I could no longer abide the church's tight-assed rejection of all things fun and sensual, its advocacy of the subjugation of women, and its intolerance of the rest of Christianity — not to mention all other religions. So in the middle of my junior year, I dug in my heels and stopped going, much to Grandma's dismay. These days, I considered myself a Bible-steeped, frightened skeptic with deeply neurotic Baptist tendencies.

The yowling of Wiley and the insistent purring of Holly greeted me at the door of my apartment. I popped popcorn for me and the cats while I resisted an urge to call Julia. Then, I searched the Sunday classifieds for a new apartment. I found a few more leads. After that, I turned in.

As soon as the lights were out, my mind started racing. I worried that I had gone too far with Gruber. Some men turn hostile after a woman reveals she is a lesbian. I hoped Gruber wasn't one of those types who — thanks to a thriving porno industry — believed that all a woman needed to go straight was one good screw, whether she wanted it or not. Still, I didn't think he got it when I told him that he was hitting close to home. And the thought of Julia also worried me. I had been out of circulation for a long time. What would I say? What would I do? I had to put her out of my mind. She was out of my league, anyway. And what would be the fallout from my note to Sargent? Would I be looking for a job come Tuesday? Would Grandma ever end the siege?

It took me three hours to fall asleep.

The alarm clock awoke me at 9:00 a.m. Thank goodness Grandma was already in the throes of her pre-Sunday school gossip session in the church parking lot. I could spend the morning in peace. I fixed coffee and toasted a pita cheese sandwich.

It was no use. The Julia obsession was not going to go away. I picked up the phone book. There were zillions of Nickels and Nichols. I would never find her. I called the newsroom.

"*Times,* Smith here." He was one of the assignment editors. He had drawn Sunday morning duty and was not happy.

"Hi, Leonard. This is Carmen Ramirez. I'm on the copy desk."

"What's up?"

"Could you do me a favor? Could you look up a phone number in the system for me? I need to get in touch with a staffer."

I heard him sigh. "Shoot."

"Julia Nichols. She works in the library."

"Spell it."

"I don't know how."

"Shit," he muttered. I could hear him typing.

"Okay. Here it is. The name's spelled N-I-C-H-O-L-S." He gruffly gave me the number.

"Thanks."

He hung up without replying.

So, at last I could call Julia. But what would I say? *I'll ad-lib — be clever, charming, spontaneous.* I felt nauseous.

I dialed the number.

After the third ring, a sleepy voice answered: "Hello?"

"Hi. Julia?"

"Uh-huh."

"This is Carmen. Carmen Ramirez. Did I wake you up?"

"Yeah. I mean I was sort of awake already."

"Oh, I'm sorry." *Oh no. I woke her up.*

"It's no problem."

"Are you sure?"

"Yeah," Julia said.

"Well," I said, "I had been wanting to call you."

"Uh-huh."

"And so I did. I don't really have an agenda."

"I'm glad you called."

"Well, good," I said. I took a deep breath. "Would you maybe like to get together for lunch or coffee or shopping or something?"

"Sure."

"Really?" *Carmen, you have just registered a Perfect Ten on the Idiot Scale.*

"Yeah. Sure," Julia said. "Did you have a time in mind?"

"No, not really," I said. *She just said yes. Think!*

"Oh. I thought you meant today."

"Today?" I said. I was in full panic.

"Yeah. I'm not busy."

She just said "today" twice. Do something. Behold, now is the accepted time. Behold, now is the day of salvation. "Well, sure. I mean, if you don't have other plans."

"No, really I don't."

"Well, why don't we meet for lunch?" *Lunch. Great! I came up with a plan.*

"I don't have a car. It will have to be within walking distance of FCU."

"I can drive. I mean, I can give you a ride in my car, if you like, that is."

"Sure," Julia said.

"How about 11:30?"

"Seems like a very lunchy time."

"Where do you live?"

"Mabel Smith Hall. You know it?"

"Yeah, sure. I'm a proud Tornado alum."

"Pull around in the front drive. I can see you from the lobby."

"Okay. Look for a navy-blue Honda Civic."

"See you soon."

I hung up the phone and squealed. Calm down, I told myself. You haven't just been invited to the Sappho Memorial High School prom by the captain of the field hockey team. You're going out to lunch with a co-worker. A co-worker who could very well be straight. I took a deep breath. I found myself humming "I Feel Pretty."

Cleanliness is important. I drew a warm bath. I threw in a generous portion of foaming bath crystals, despite the fact that Jane declared it politically incorrect to do so. You are eradicating your natural smells and replacing them with male-defined attractive scents, she had told me. To hell with that. The crystals turned the water blue and foamy, and I liked it that way.

I climbed in the tub. The cats climbed up on the rim to watch. Wiley batted at the foam while Holly crouched and looked concerned. You guys. Can't a girl bathe in peace?

They were unfazed. They remained with me throughout the lengthy bathing process, although Holly eventually got over his concern and took a nap on the bath mat.

I patted myself dry. I opened my closet and unearthed the Chanel gift set Raúl had sent me for Christmas a couple of years ago. I used just a splash of the body lotion and a whisper of the No. 5 perfume.

And now, to the matter of clothing. By this point, I was ready to mince around in high heels and a tight leather miniskirt, but fortunately, I didn't own that type of gear. I opted for some pleated light gray cotton slacks, a white oxford shirt, and ox-blood penny loafers. Uncharacteristically, I pressed my slacks and shirt. By the time I finished dolling up (I even used the hair dryer), I looked like a young Republican Hispanic dyke and smelled like a French floozy. I gave myself the once-over in the mirror. The top two buttons of my shirt were undone. That would never do. I buttoned the second button. It was pointless to show off my boobs to a woman who might not even be a lesbian.

I glanced at my watch — a dressy Seiko Grandma had given me for my college graduation, despite her hatred of the Japanese — as I parked in the

U-shaped drive in front of Mabel Smith Hall. I was only ten minutes early. I fiddled with the radio. News, preachers, country twangers, and pop fluff dominated the airwaves. I switched it off. If I had sprung for a cassette deck, I wouldn't be so nervous now. I was wrong to think I could live without it. It would be nice to punch in some Heart, Led Zep, or David Bowie right about now. Instead, I had to listen to the traffic roar past the campus and the cicadas humming in the bushes.

I was not the portrait of sophisticated composure. My palms were very wet, and my legs were shaky. I checked out my hair in the rearview mirror. It was holding up surprisingly well. The humidity must have been low today.

Exactly five minutes early, Julia came bounding down the front steps. She wore red, blue, and green plaid walking shorts and a green polo shirt. I tried to ignore the fact that she was not wearing a bra. As she jogged to the car, I avoided the sight of her well-tanned legs.

"Hi there," she said. Mismatched earrings — a small gold hoop and a black bead — adorned her ears. "Come here often?"

"Hi, get in," I said. "Let's get rolling."

Civics are very small cars — subcompacts to be exact. As soon as she got in, I could smell her. I could smell that she was freshly showered and clean. But I could also smell her own personal scent. And I liked it. This was going to be tough. I was trembling.

"Ooh, you smell great. Is that Chanel No. 5?" Julia asked.

I must have smelled like a French whore. "Yeah. I think I overdid it a little."

"Chanel No. 5 is my absolute favorite," she said.

By this time, I must have been blushing. "So, where to?" I said, twirling my key chain around in my fingers.

"I'll eat anything. I don't mind."

I started the car without saying anything. I wanted to scream. Finally, I regained control. "How about the Fifteenth Street Diner? Good food and plenty of it."

"Never been there before, but I'd be glad to try it," Julia said.

As I slipped the stick shift into reverse, my hand accidentally brushed her knee. A chill ran through me. "Oh, sorry," I said. "Watch your knee, I mean. It's awfully tight quarters in here."

I drove to the diner without saying anything else, concentrating on the traffic — not Julia's lovely smell or gorgeous knees.

We got there just in time. At this time of the day, only the heathens were eating lunch. As soon as the churches let out, the place would be packed. The diner had been moderately successful for years because of its cheap, tasty down-home fare; however, when a new owner took over a couple of years back, he turned the place into a fifties-style diner with ponytailed waitresses in poodle skirts, with chrome and glass walls and large aqua vinyl booths, and fifties music on the sound system. Happily, the food had remained the same. As a result, neighborhood customers — slightly perturbed by all the hype —

continued to frequent the place, but so did a new crowd — of college students, yuppies, and other trendy types.

Our waitress was the legendary Jo, who had been waiting tables at that diner since before I was born. In her mid-sixties, she wore makeup heavy enough for Kabuki theater and sported a giant platinum bouffant with a tiny ponytail. She guided us to a corner booth with the authority of a Marine drill instructor.

We ordered cheeseburgers, fries and gravy, and cherry limeades. Jo brought our order out in fifteen minutes.

"This looks great," Julia said. "So, is this your hangout?"

"I've come here since I was a kid," I said. I gestured to the waitress. "Jo has been here since the dawn of time."

Julia let out a long breath and stretched. She looked nice when she stretched. "It's really nice to get away from campus. When you don't have a car, it kind of limits you. I get out on my bike or catch rides from friends, but it's not the same."

"No car? That's un-American."

"Yeah, well tell me about it," Julia said. "Bob and Naomi just never got around to getting their little girl a car. I don't even know how to drive."

"Bob and Naomi?"

"My parents. Bob and Naomi Nichols of Wilton, Arkansas. Population ten thousand. Sa-lute."

"Wilton. That's up in the Ozarks, right?"

"Yep. A beautiful place to grow up. Anyway, this

guy I was dating was going to teach me how to drive, but we haven't been seeing each other very much lately."

I felt a sledgehammer hit my chest. A boyfriend. She was straight after all.

Julia continued. "I just feel incredibly inept being almost twenty-one and being unable to drive."

I pulled myself together. I heard myself asking: "So what's the story on your boyfriend?"

"Oh, I don't know. I think the relationship is just running out of steam. I just don't want to see him anymore. I just haven't gotten around to telling him."

I stared at my cherry limeade. So, she was straight. Most people were straight. I felt sick to my stomach.

"Are you all right?" Julia said.

"To tell you the truth, I'm feeling a little queasy," I said. I felt like a fool. I was all dolled up for this straight woman. God, I hated my life.

"Oh, I am sorry. If you'd like to come back to my room, I could fetch you some Maalox or something. My mother sends me drugs all the time. She believes in a very complete first-aid kit."

"No, really, that's okay," I said. I didn't know how much longer I could keep a grip on my emotions. "Listen, I have to get out of here. I'm really not well. Mind if I take you back?"

"No. Not at all."

I paid the check and escorted Julia to the car. I drove back to FCU without talking to her.

"Listen, Carmen, are you okay? I'm worried about you," she said as I pulled up in front of her residence hall.

"Yeah. I'm fine. I should just lie down. I'll be okay." *Get away from her. Don't fall apart.*

"You want to come up? I can make you a cup of tea."

"Really, I'm just fine."

She kept staring at me. "Did I offend you?"

Jesus Christ. These straight girls never want to let you escape with your dignity. "No. I just need to go."

I watched her walk up the stairs. I pulled out of the driveway and onto College Street. You're okay, I told myself. It was just a misunderstanding. You took a risk. It didn't pay off. You're okay.

I headed for the nearest convenience store — a Speedy Petey — and bought two packs of Marlboros. I hadn't had a cigarette for months. But fuck it, I needed a smoke.

CHAPTER 4

That weekend, the cigarettes gave me little satisfaction. I threw them away after going through half a pack. I let the answering machine take my calls. Julia called twice, but I didn't return her calls. I didn't feel I could be civil. I was too angry at myself.

Tuesday, I returned to work. I had pulled myself together. I could manage being polite to Julia. After all, she had merely been friendly and open. I had been at fault for misreading the signals.

I logged on at my usual terminal and braced

myself for the worst. I was sure Blazer wouldn't react well to my note. Sure enough, he had sent me this reply.

Carmen:
    Jeff and I have spent long hours researching this case, and we feel confident with the conclusions we have drawn. Sargent agrees.
    Ron

I drew in a deep breath. I had followed newsroom protocol to the letter, but something was not right here. I decided to confront Blazer.

A bland-looking man with a salt-and-pepper bowl cut, Blazer sat at his terminal at the assignment desk. He didn't look up when I walked over.

"Ron?"

He continued staring at his screen with his yellow-brown eyes.

"Ron?" I said again, more forcefully.

He looked up at me without saying anything.

"I'm Carmen Ramirez."

He looked back down at his terminal.

"I have to talk to you."

"What about?" His voice was flat, without emotion.

"The series."

He sighed. "Is there a new problem?"

"No, Ron." Why was he always so difficult?

"Then what?"

"I think we're being unfair to Diane Barrett. I don't know whether she's innocent, but our series doesn't even entertain the possibility that there could be another suspect. We immediately label her as guilty because she's a lesbian with a drinking problem."

He continued to stare at his screen.

This asshole was ignoring me. "Well?" I said.

"You have made your objections clear," he said. "But the decision has been made. You are not the reporter on this case. You are not the editor in charge of this case. You are a copy editor. A fledgling copy editor at that. Your job is to check style, punctuation, and grammar, and to point out problems with content."

"I know what my job is, Ron," I said. I noticed several people look up from their computer terminals. I took a deep breath.

"Then I suggest you stick to it," he said in the same monotone.

I stormed away from Blazer's desk. I knew that if there was to be any change in the series, I would have to dig up more information. But what could I do? And what was I looking for?

I headed back to the library and steeled myself to face Julia. Gorgeous as ever, she was sitting at a computer terminal.

"Hi," I said.

"I called you. Twice," she said, her voice hurt and angry.

"Sorry. I didn't feel like talking to anyone," I said.

Julia glared at me. "You're pretty tough to figure out."

"Sorry," I said. I tried to muster my most professional voice. "I need you to look up some information for me."

"Of course," she said.

"I need you to look through the microfilm archives for the clips on the Rev. Bobby Ray Metcalf's wife. I don't know the first name. He has two daughters, one of them dead. I just need to know who produced these children and what happened to her."

"I'm sure you're aware that you can search for her yourself in the database."

She was pissing me off. I took a breath. "Yes. I've already tried that. I can't find a trace of her."

"It will take a while if you don't have the first name. And I have a lot of other work that takes priority over this."

She was definitely angry. "I guess I'll just have to do it on my own time. Thanks for your help," I said.

I walked out without waiting to see her reaction.

That night, after my shift, Sargent asked to see me.

"What's up?" I said as I approached his litter-strewn desk.

He swiveled his chair around and looked me straight in the eye. "Ron tells me you two had a run-in over the series."

"Yeah. We did," I said calmly. I didn't want to show him how defensive I was feeling.

"Carmen, whether you like it or not, you're going to have to drop this thing," he said emphatically.

"Ralph, this series is a bunch of gay-bashing nonsense. I won't back off."

He paused. "God damn it. I need someone who can work with the assignment desk."

"Ron refuses to be worked with. He wants everything his way or not at all," I said angrily.

"Carmen, he outranks you. If there is a problem, you tell me. If I go with him, that's the end of the discussion. Do you understand?"

"Even if you happen to be dead wrong?" I said. I knew I'd gone too far.

Sargent's face turned purple. "This is my copy desk, and we do things my way," he shouted. He took a deep breath. "You're off the series."

I looked at him without replying. I knew my job was hanging by the most frayed of threads.

He continued bellowing: "And let me warn you — you need to learn how things run in this newsroom. And you need to learn to think with your mouth shut. If you don't, you're not going to last in this business. You've got to earn your stripes before you can act like me. Right now, you're a buck private," he said. "I'm going out for a drink. I suggest you do the same."

He stood up, and I watched him walk out of the newsroom.

"Damn you, bastard," I said, after he was gone. I was trembling. "I'll show you who's off the case."

Sargent and Blazer didn't know me very well. I was as stubborn as they came when I was in a corner. My grandmother, the church, and the public school system had done everything in their power to make me into something I would never be: a quiet, submissive, God-fearing, heterosexual Southern Baptist. You have to possess a strong will to stand up to that onslaught.

Sargent and Blazer were in for the fight of their lives.

An hour after Sargent's scolding, I was still trying to figure out the library's system of organization. The chronologically arranged microfilms of every edition of the paper would be hopelessly time-consuming. After searching through long aisles of gray metal filing cabinets, I found another set of records — microfilm clips arranged by topic. I searched through a card catalog and at last found the clips on Metcalf's wife, LaDonna.

LaDonna Metcalf was out of the picture, all right. There were two stories on her. One was an obituary. She had died in 1973, while little Rebecca was still in diapers. The obit was brief, its headline: LADONNA METCALF, 25; MINISTER'S WIFE. It cited a longtime illness as the cause of death, outlined her brief career as a wife and mother, and listed her survivors and their hometowns. The only other story on Mrs. Metcalf was from six months earlier. She had been involved in a single-car early morning crash in Frontier City and had been admitted to a hospital for unspecified injuries.

That sounded fishy. People involved in single-car crashes were usually drunk or high on drugs or suicidal. Or all three. Unless the roads were icy or rainy. The crash had happened in March; there might have been ice on the roads then, but it was unlikely. Spring usually came early in Oklahoma. I checked the weather pages for the week of the wreck. They showed no rain or snow.

I made printouts and headed home.

Late that night as I lay in bed, I drove all thoughts of Sargent's fury out of my head by plotting my strategy. I needed to talk to Diane Barrett's school colleagues. I needed to know who she was and what made her tick. And I needed to find out more about Rebecca's life. Had there been any sex offenders around her? And I had to find out more about Mrs. Metcalf. Of course, I could contact the survivors, but that would be tough. What would make these people — probably a bunch of religious fanatics — want to talk to a copy editor about their long-dead relative, who might have been a suicide? If I were in their place, I had to admit, I wouldn't give a nosy journalist the time of day.

Rebecca Metcalf and I both had lost our mothers at an early age. But at least I'd had a mother surrogate around to raise me. What would my life have been like if I had been raised by a father — and a preacher at that? My own father had always been so distant: a voice on the telephone, cards and gifts at birthdays and holidays. It must have been lonely for her.

I made a mental note to follow up on the survivors. I would think of a strategy when I called.

The next morning, I was awakened by the ringing of the phone.

"It's Julia."

I sat up. "Yes?"

"What the hell is going on?"

"I beg your pardon?"

"I'm not used to having people despise me."

"I don't despise you," I said.

"Like hell," she said. "We were starting to be friends. And then, all of a sudden, you develop a stomach ache and turn into some kind of bitch. What is the problem?"

I took a breath. I would be damned if I was going to let her drag out my feelings at, according to my clock, 10:30 in the morning. "Julia, I was at work late last night, looking up stuff on that preacher's wife in the microfilm archives. I didn't get to bed until late. You woke me up. I haven't even had my coffee."

"Look, I'm sorry, but this is really eating me. I'm not used to being shunned. Tell me what's going on."

"There's nothing to tell."

"Bullshit."

"Please," I said. "I told you: There's nothing to tell."

There was a pause on Julia's end. "Carmen, you weren't sick at your stomach that day. You had the same thing I did, and I didn't get sick. All of a sudden, you just turned on me."

Julia would make a great prosecuting attorney. "I don't have any obligation to explain myself to you," I said softly.

"No, I don't suppose so. I guess I just misread the situation."

"Julia, I didn't mean to hurt your feelings."

"Well, they're still hurt."

Should I tell her? Maybe she already knew and

was just playing stupid. I didn't want to be vulnerable.

"All right, Julia." I took a deep breath. "If you must know, I am a lesbian. All right?"

I waited for her to respond, but she said nothing. I said, "I was interested in getting to know you better. But I wasn't out to leap on you and attack you or anything. At the diner, you started talking about a boyfriend. At that point, I felt stupid because I had misread the situation, so I decided to bail out with my dignity intact. But you, Miss Nichols, refused to let me do so. So there you have it."

There was a long silence.

"Julia, I want to hang up now."

"Can we start over?"

I paused. "I don't know if that's such a good idea," I said.

"Carmen, look here, I like you a lot. I feel comfortable with you. I enjoy being around you. And you like me, too, right?"

Don't answer, I told myself. "Yes, I said."

"So why not just start over, with a clean slate?"

"I don't know. What are the ground rules?"

"There are no ground rules, as far as I'm concerned."

What was this woman up to? "Okay, Julia. I'll play along."

"Let me make it up to you. I'll treat you to dinner. I promise I won't talk about boys. Besides, I'm not seeing him anymore. Let's make it this weekend. Maybe Sunday?"

"All right. Sunday it is."

"Meet me at the dorm at six."

"Sure."

I looked at the cats, asleep at the foot of the bed. "How can you sleep at a time like this?" I said.

I arrived in the newsroom early so I could contact people connected with the Metcalf case.

According to the obit, Jeannie Moffett, LaDonna Metcalf's mother, had lived in Arrowhead, a small town east of Frontier City, at the time of her daughter's death. I called up directory assistance and tracked down a J. Moffett who still lived there.

I cleared my throat and dialed.

A tired voice answered.

"Hi, my name is," I paused, "Carla Sullivan. I'm a reporter for the *Frontier City Herald*." I used an alias and the name of the competition in case she got vindictive and wanted to report me.

"Honey, I already take your paper."

"No, this isn't about a subscription, ma'am. Is this Mrs. Jeannie Moffett?"

"Yes it is," she said warily.

"Are you the mother of the late LaDonna Metcalf?"

"Yes, I am. What is this all about?"

"Well, ma'am, we are doing some research about the murder of your granddaughter, and we'd like to know a little bit about her mother."

"I don't have to talk to you."

And with that, the phone went dead.

Stupid, stupid, stupid. I would have to drive out to Arrowhead if I was going to get anything out of Mrs. Moffett.

Next, I attempted to track down Myra Hawkins and Ruby Weller. Both were unlisted so I called the school. The secretary was of no help. Dr. Hawkins and Ms. Weller were unavailable and under no circumstances could their home phone numbers be given out. I was annoyed by the secretary's snotty tone. It was probably some strategy to intimidate parents. I left messages for both women.

Later that night, Gruber handled the Barrett series while I endured my punishment — editing wire stories for the farm page, scintillating pieces about worming cattle and dipping sheep. I couldn't blame Sargent for punishing me. I had defied him. For now, I had to lay low.

The next day, I set out early to drive the thirty miles east to Arrowhead. Despite the late-summer heat, I had dressed in a navy pantsuit and a flimsy, femmy white blouse, my accessories large red button earrings with matching scarf, pumps, and bag. I had even put on a hint of makeup. I wanted to look as professional as possible. The cats were extremely helpful during my preparations, nearly tripping me several times as they constantly rubbed at my legs.

Highway 33, a four-lane highway, became a two-lane blacktop outside of the Frontier City limits. The road followed a winding path as the city gave way to rolling farm country, with its tractors, pickup trucks, and aging barns set in the middle of wide fields of alfalfa, beans, and wheat.

I didn't know much about Arrowhead. Grandma and I had driven through the town when we were on our way to visit our Arkansas kin, but I had no idea how to find my way around. All I could do was get there and ask and hope no one resented me for my Japanese car with its Frontier County license plate.

Highway 33 became Main Street as it entered Arrowhead, a drab red-brick town dating from the time of Indian Territory. I pulled up in front of Fred's Gibble gas station, with its Depression-era pumps, and headed for the office.

A toothless old chap wearing a filthy ballcap looked up from his tiny black-and-white television. He was watching "Bonanza." Hoss was duking it out with three bad guys. Toothless spat tobacco juice into a rusty Folgers coffee can.

"What can I do you for?" he said.

"Hi there," I said in my most folksy voice. "I'm looking for Hillman Road."

"Who you looking for up there?"

"Mrs. Moffett's place."

"Moffett place. Hmm. You kin to her?"

"Friend of the family," I said.

He peered out at my car. "Jeannie never mentioned having no friends up to Frontier City."

"Can you tell me how to get there?" I was suffocating inside my polyester-blend chain mail.

"Sure thing, little lady. Just stay on Main till you pass the old Bible Church on the left. Shoot up that road, and that's Hillman. Jeannie's place is the white house with the wishing well up front. Can't miss it."

"Thank you, sir."

"Any time, pretty lady." He returned to eyeing the adventures of the Cartwrights.

Toothless's directions led me straight to Hillman, a poorly maintained gravel road, and Mrs. Moffett's home, a small frame house badly in need of a paint job. I pulled into the drive. I rang the bell four times before a haggard woman appeared, wearing a pink curler cap and a faded housecoat in a floral print — pink cabbage roses and green leaves on a white background.

"Yes," she said.

My heart was pounding. What business did I have digging into this woman's affairs? "Mrs. Moffett?"

"Yes?"

"I'm Carla Sullivan. I called you yesterday."

Her face reddened, and she started to slam the door.

"Wait a minute," I said. "Please, just let me talk to you for a second."

She folded her arms and stared at me through the screen door.

"Mrs. Moffett, I know this is painful, but I want to ask you a couple of questions about your granddaughter's death."

She glowered at me. "Don't you vultures ever get enough?"

"I'm not out to make you or your family look bad. I'm sorry if the press has hurt you."

"I don't need your pity."

"Ma'am, just a couple of questions — I've come all the way from Frontier City to talk to you."

Mrs. Moffett shrugged, but she didn't slam the door.

"Did Rebecca ever let on that she was

uncomfortable around a teacher, a neighbor, a baby sitter, perhaps?"

Mrs. Moffett glared at me for a long time. "She never said a thing to me about it. Don't you think I'd have done something?"

"Yes, of course you would have," I said. "Did your daughter ever suffer from any problems like depression?"

Mrs. Moffett's face contorted into a mask of grief and rage. "Who the hell do you think you are? You wanna write something? Write this down: My LaDonna was a fine Christian. A popular, happy girl. Homecoming queen. She could have married any boy in town. Went to LTU on a music scholarship. Talented, played the piano like an angel. Any hymn, she knew it by heart. She had two beautiful little girls, a deep faith in the Lord Jesus Christ. How dare you pry into my family's affairs? The Lord took LaDonna and Rebecca home. That's all we know."

Mrs. Moffett drew in her breath and slammed the door.

My face was stinging with humiliation as I walked to the car.

As soon as I arrived back, I checked the answering machine. Dr. Hawkins had indeed called me back. There was nothing from Weller.

I quickly called the number Hawkins had left for me.

"Dr. Hawkins," a humorless voice answered.

"Yes," I said. "My name is Carla Sullivan. I'm a

journalist. I'd like to speak to you about the Barrett case. Could we arrange an interview?"

"I have already spoken to the press numerous times. I can't see the usefulness of another interview."

"Please, Dr. Hawkins," I said. "I just have a few loose ends to tie up. I know you're busy and that this case has dragged on. I promise I won't waste your time."

"Very well, Miss Sullivan," she said.

We arranged to meet the following week.

As I ditched my clothes, washed off my makeup, and changed into comfortable clothes for work, I worried about what I had started. I wasn't an experienced reporter. I had done some soft reporting duty for my college newspaper, and that was it. For the rest of my brief journalism career I had been a clerk or copy editor. And I was no Mike Wallace when it came to asking tough questions.

Still, I had to try to speak with the Rev. Metcalf. Surely I could gain some clue from him about what had happened with his wife and daughter.

I called the Southside Tabernacle and made an appointment to speak with the Reverend the following week. I left another message for Ruby Weller at the school.

On Sunday, I decided to watch the Rev. Metcalf in action. So I dolled up in my wholesome navy suit again and drove out to the far South Side. Like all good fundamentalist Christians, I carried my black, soft-leather, chain-reference, red-letter-edition Bible, my name emblazoned on it in gold. The Bible was a gift from Grandma after I had made my Profession of Faith and then had been baptized at twelve following a grueling week at church camp.

I parked under a shade tree in the sprawling lot, which sat in the middle of a heavily wooded tract. I was early. I would make the 11:00 a.m. service with no trouble.

The sanctuary was an imposing, octagonal structure, flanked by two wings of offices and classrooms. Its white stucco walls were punctuated with huge stained-glass windows, three stories high. When I entered the building, I was greeted by a cheerful, balding, middle-aged white man in white slacks, plaid sports coat, and yellow shirt. In lieu of a tie, he wore a cross made out of nails around his neck. He carried a handful of church bulletins.

"Good morning, sister," Mr. Sports Coat said, pumping my hand with evangelical vigor. "Jesus loves you, and so do I."

"Thank you," I said.

I took a bulletin and headed for the first balcony. The huge church had two.

The pews were not long and hard like those at the Fourteenth Street Baptist Church, but instead, were folded-up, padded theater seats, upholstered in a plush burgundy fabric that matched the carpeting.

The bulletin, full-color and printed on slick paper, showed off just how much money the church had. My old church mimeographed its bulletins on the cheapest paper it could find. The front photo showed a night shot of the tabernacle, with light streaming

71

through the abstract designs on its stained-glass windows. The back cover displayed a studio shot of Metcalf in a prayerful pose.

Inside, the bulletin had all the usual information: staff, baptisms, marriages, deaths, and sick people to pray for. It listed last week's attendance — 5,432, counting all those reached by the church's satellite ministries in nursing homes, jails, and hospitals. And it listed last week's collections: a whopping $35,879.15. Underneath that figure, was the statement: "We walk by faith and not by sight as a tithing church." Doing some rough calculations, I figured that the church might be hauling in over two million dollars a year since summer was usually slow for collections and attendance. Their coffers must be bulging, come Christmas and Easter, when all the guilt-racked back-sliders show up and attempt to make up for another year of missed church attendance.

I moved on to the order of worship for that week's services: hymns to be sung by congregation and choir; scripture passages to be read; sermon themes. Rachel Metcalf was to be a featured soloist. "How Great Thou Art" — a gospel chestnut sung by everyone from Elvis to George Beverly Shea — was to be her solo.

I scanned the crowd streaming into the church. They looked affluent, each carrying his or her own Bible. Men in expensive suits. Women in the latest fashions. Children well-groomed and wholesome. Not a brown face in the bunch, save mine, and I was not all that brown. Without knowing my name, people usually assumed I was white, perhaps with a

Cherokee grandma. Raúl would have definitely stuck out in this crowd.

Only in its lily-white composition did this church resemble my old congregation. At the Fourteenth Street Baptist Church, the people there dressed up, to be sure, but in threadbare J.C. Penney suits and dresses sewed at home on the Singer. We met in a plain white room with hardwood pews, yellow plexiglass windows, and linoleum floor. And the collection and attendance never came close to the success at this church. Maybe four hundred people would come on a good week. And the collection would reach maybe three grand, tops. The tabernacle would be the envy of any man of the cloth.

The lights dimmed. The service began. Much to my surprise, a small orchestra rose from a platform beneath the floor in front of the pulpit. The congregation stood.

I heard a rolling sound. A timpanist pounding his drums. A trumpet called out high, piercing, staccato notes. I started sweating nervously. This service was going to be way too intense for my taste.

The choir, wearing lush robes that matched the carpet and upholstery, filed into the loft, behind the pulpit. They sang, at full fortissimo, "All Hail the Power of Jesus' Name." Members of the congregation joined in, with some of the old-fashioned Pentecostals shaking tambourines or clapping.

I'd made a huge mistake. I had to get out of there. This place was as weird as they come. I looked to my left. The man next to me — a well-dressed businessman — swayed to the music. It would be unwise to bother him. I turned to my right. An extremely dignified-looking woman in her fifties stood calmly next to me.

"Excuse me," I said, trying to speak loudly enough to be heard without disrupting the clamorous worship. "I need to leave."

Just then, tears began streaming down her face. She started moaning and muttering what sounded like gibberish to me. Perhaps she was acknowledging me and had some sort of extreme speech impediment.

"I beg your pardon?" I said.

She continued her singsong stream of words. She was speaking in tongues.

I flashed back to my Sunday school days. Mrs. Lofton, my Junior 5 teacher, telling us that unknown tongues were only for the time of the Apostles, and people who claimed to speak in tongues today were either hysterical or possessed by demons.

I shivered as I watched the woman next to me. Could she be possessed? Get a grip, Carmen, I told myself. You should have never disobeyed Grandma by secretly reading *The Exorcist* back in the sixth grade. You've been scared shitless of demons ever since. I took a deep breath and attempted to calm down.

The opening song went on for a good fifteen minutes that seemed more like an hour. If they carried on like this on a regular Sunday, Easter must be one hell of a show.

There were several more hymns and introductory remarks from subordinate ministers. My claustrophobia was growing by the minute. At last, Bobby Ray Metcalf rose to the podium. Dressed immaculately in a dark, double-breasted Italian suit, he looked more like a businessman than a preacher. Grandma would have called him a flashy character.

"How many of you are glad to be in the House of the Lord? Say amen," he said in a polished, booming baritone.

A thunderous amen arose from the congregation. Everyone but me.

His voice changed to a weeping urgency. "A lot of you know that my wife, LaDonna, and, two years ago, my little Rebecca were taken home to be with the Lord. But you know what? The Lord Jesus left me with one joy in my life, and that's my little Rachel."

The congregation began applauding. So, at last they were going to bring her out.

He waited for the applause to die down. "And now, my little girl Rachel is going to sing for you. She's a freshman in the music program at LTU. Let's give her a big welcome. It's been a long time since she sang in front of this congregation."

The applause swelled again. Good God, what didn't make these people respond? They were like a bunch of trained seals. I had to get out of there.

From the choir loft, a small figure made her way down to the pulpit. Rev. Metcalf smiled and embraced his daughter.

Rachel held up her hand. The congregation halted its applause. I strained to make out her expression. She seemed to be smiling. She spoke in a tentative voice: "I want to thank all of you for standing with me in prayer through my time of sickness. God bless you all."

The applause began again. Rachel smiled and nodded to the organist, who replied with an old-time gospel introduction to "How Great Thou Art." All the shyness disappeared as the young woman launched into the hymn. An heir to her mothers musical skill, she sang with command and feeling. As the hymn closed, the worshipers, many of them weeping, gave her a standing ovation.

"Thank you," she said, her sheepishness returning. "God love you all." With that, she retreated to the choir.

I simply couldn't sit through any more. At this point, the service had already been going on an hour. When the next hymn started, I started coughing. I coughed fiercely, like a tubercular patient on her deathbed.

The Unknown Tongues lady looked at me with concern. "Are you okay?" she said.

I was relieved that, this time, I could understand her. "I just need a drop of water, I think."

She gave way and let me out of the row. I reminded myself that I was still in church and shouldn't bolt.

In the lobby, I was greeted again by Mr. Sports Coat. "Everything all right, sister?"

"Just this nasty cough. Think I'd better head home."

"Brother Bobby Ray lays hands on people at the evening service if you want to come back then. The Lord will cast out that demon cough."

"Oh yeah, I'll sure do that," I said. "By the way, I'm new to your church here. What was wrong with Rachel? How has she been sick?"

"She had to be up in Vinewood Hospital for quite a while after her sister died. Some sort of depression or something. Poor gal. But our prayer warriors prayed that demon of despair right out of her. Praise God."

"Amen," I said. "Well, goodbye."

"Goodbye, sister. You come back now. You be sure to fill out that visitor's card. And call our prayer warriors anytime with your needs. We just lay them at the foot of the cross."

"Thank you," I said. With that, I headed toward the door before Mr. Sports Coat could cast any demons out of me. As soon as I hit the sidewalk, I sprinted for the car.

Back home again, I pondered my date with Julia. I was torn between anger and excitement. I reached for the phone.

"Charles, it's me, Carmen."

"Oh, hi, sweetie," he said. I could tell he was disappointed. "How are you?"

"Fine, I guess," I said. "How are things going with you and the salesman?"

"Roger's been on the road forever. I haven't heard from him in two whole days. I'm dying."

"I'm sorry. Why don't you just call him?"

"He's somewhere between here and Bakersfield. He said he'd call me when he has time. I just have to believe he will."

"I'm sure he will. He's probably just swamped with work."

"I hope so. In fact, I thought he was calling when the phone rang. I found myself singing 'Let It

Please Be Him.' You don't think I'm turning into Vikki Carr, do you?"

"I certainly hope not."

"So what's on your mind, sweetheart?"

"Oh, Charlie, you're having such a bad time. I don't want to lay any more on you."

"Nonsense. Misery delights in company. You should know that."

"I'll make it brief, since you're waiting to hear from your beau. It's Julia. I know she's straight. She mentioned a boyfriend. I told her I'm a lesbian, but she still says she wants to go out with me. You know, in a friendly way."

"Of course you told her no?"

"We're going out tonight."

"Oh God, Carmen."

"I don't know what to do."

"Call her now. Break it off. Wait till a nice lesbian who has her head together comes along. Believe me. You don't need this heartache."

"I know you're right."

"You bet I am, sweetheart."

"There's also some unpleasant stuff going on at work right now. I was assigned to edit a series on Diane Barrett."

"You mean the killer lesbian teacher?"

"Yeah. I think our coverage is unfair, you know, really homophobic, and I sounded off about it. So my boss pulled me off the series. He's really pissed at me, and, in a way, I really can't blame him. You know?"

"Oh, shit, Carmen. You're in Oklahoma, not

Greenwich Village. Be careful. Being radically queer there can get you in a lot of trouble."

"Listen, don't I know it. Please take care of yourself. And don't waste your life sitting by the phone. Put on the answering machine and go out, for God's sake. You're in Berkeley, right next to the gay capital of the world. Go out and enjoy it."

"All right, Carmen. Take care."

I knew he wasn't going to follow my advice. And I had no intention of canceling on Julia or backing off on the Barrett case.

Later that night, Julia and I sat in strained silence as we hunched over mugs of beer at a pizza parlor near campus. Julia had picked the spot because it didn't mind serving beer to patrons under twenty-one. I was feeling edgy and peevish because I couldn't control my feelings for Julia. Being around her still made my pulse quicken. She looked as beautiful as ever, wearing baggy khaki walking shorts and a bright multi-colored floral Hawaiian print shirt over a dark blue tank top. Her green eyes shone in the candlelight. I had gone to less trouble for this date. I had put on a pair of Levis and a plain red T-shirt. Well, at least the red made my dark black eyes look more dramatic.

Finally, Julia said: "Maybe this wasn't such a good idea."

"Oh, I don't know. Let's just give it some time."

Our pizza came, and we ate in silence.

I couldn't stand the tension. As we waited for the check to come, I decided to bring matters to a head. "Maybe we should go out and do something."

"Like what?"

"I don't know. Maybe shoot some pool or something like that."

"Okay, Julia said. Let's go."

We headed for the car. "Do you have a fake ID?"

"Yeah. Why?"

Sick of all these games, I put it all on the line. "Well, there's a women's bar we could go to. We could shoot pool or play video games, and there aren't any men there to bug you. But Crystal's really strict about IDs."

"A bar just for women?"

"Yeah. Lesbians," I said, watching her reaction. She seemed a little flustered. "If you would be uncomfortable, we don't have to go there."

"No, I would go there with you — if it's not gross or anything."

I paused, then backed off. She wasn't interested. "No, never mind. It was a bad idea. You probably would find it gross."

"Is this some kind of weird test?"

"No," I said. Actually, it probably was a weird test. "Not at all. I asked you and you said you wouldn't be comfortable. So we won't go."

"Whatever," Julia said angrily. "I didn't mean anything by the gross comment."

"I'm sure you didn't."

"Look, Carmen, I'm happy to do anything you want. I just don't like the feeling that I'm on trial."

"Just forget it." She was way ahead of me.

"Stop playing games. Drive to the bar or take me home. All right?" Julia said.

"Fine," I said.

We drove silently across town to Crystal's. The parking lot was deserted.

"I don't think it's open," Julia said.

"Maybe not." I pulled up to the door. Sure enough, the sign on the window said CLOSED.

"Now what?" Julia said.

"I could have sworn they'd be open. Maybe Crystal was taking the night off."

"You want to come back to my room?" Julia offered.

She was trying, unsuccessfully, to look calm. I must have looked even worse.

"I have a bottle of wine, purchased with my very own phony ID. We could play cards. Or watch TV. I have my own set. It's a small screen, but it's color."

"What about your roommate?"

"I have a single."

Cards, TV, and wine in her single room. Despite all my efforts at self-control, my heart pounded wildly and I started to blush. I was queasy, despite the fact that I'd only had one mug of weak Oklahoma 3.2 percent beer that had worn off long ago.

You wanted to take her to a lesbian bar, I lectured myself. Now she wants you to come to her room. For once, try not to behave like a complete neurotic. Do something. Don't analyze it to death. Just say yes. "Sure, all right, if you like."

* * * * *

We made our way past the lobby of Mabel Smith Hall to a set of double doors.

I froze. "I don't want to ruin your reputation by going to your room."

She stared at me. "God, are you always so dramatic?"

I shrugged. She was right. This wasn't *The Well of Loneliness.* I forced myself to laugh.

"Don't worry about it. People are in and out of here all the time. Nobody will care. And even if they do, I don't."

So I'd just go and chat. It was no big deal. I followed her to the second floor. Her room was at the top of the stairs. On the door, No. 201, was a pink construction paper rose with her name on it.

"Geez, this is cute," I said.

"The resident assistants make them for all the doors."

We walked in. The room gave new meaning to the word "tiny." There was barely enough room for a twin bed, desk, bookcase, wardrobe, sink, and mini refrigerator. Julia had decorated the walls with travel posters for San Francisco, New York, New Orleans, and Miami.

"Are you a world traveler?" I said, pointing at the posters.

"My cousin Raylene is a flight attendant for American," she said. "She gave me all these when I went off to school."

"Nice," I said.

She gestured toward the bed. "Sit down. I'll get you something to drink."

I sat on the bed, which was made up with a

homemade quilt — predominantly green and white, with red tulips. "This quilt is pretty. Did your mom make it?"

"She sure did."

Julia handed me a white plastic cup stenciled with *FCU, Home of the Fighting Tornadoes.*

I took a sip of the white wine. Cheap but not unbearable.

"Sorry about the cup and the wine. They're the best I have."

"They're fine. Stop apologizing," I said. "It's not like I'm the Queen of England. My apartment isn't much bigger than this. I bet you couldn't find two matching cups or dishes in the place. Everything I own is from my grandmother or flea markets, except the really deluxe stuff, which is from K-mart. Hell, the only reason I live as good as I do is that I get a deal on the rent. It's an apartment over my grandmother's garage."

"You mention your grandmother all the time," Julia commented.

"She raised me. My mother died when I was just a baby. My father is up in New York City. Runs a travel agency with one of his brothers. He didn't want to raise me. I guess he didn't think he could. So he sent me to live with Grandma Sullivan. Grandpa died shortly after Raúl married my mom. The doctors said heart attack, but according to my grandmother, the sight of his fair, red-headed girl walking down the aisle with a Puerto Rican did him in."

"Holy smokes."

"I'll say. I don't know how she felt about having

this little brown baby dumped on her doorstep. But she's always treated me well. I mean, as well as she can treat anybody."

I realized that I had started to babble — a sure sign of nerves. I finished off the wine.

"More?" Julia said.

"Nah. I better not. I'm driving. Besides, I'm running off at the mouth."

"I was enjoying your story."

I didn't reply.

"Would you like to see some pictures of my family?"

"Sure."

She pulled a huge blue album from a shelf and then sat next to me on the bed. My heart was pumping fiercely. *Calm yourself, girl. She's just going to show you some pictures.*

The album began with a shot of Naomi and Bob Nichols in front of Nichols' Hardware and Lumber. Both were wearing nail aprons, ballcaps, and sweat shirts with the store's name on it. Naomi was a slim woman with light brown hair. Bob was a burly blond who looked like he could have been a boxer.

"My mom and dad's business," Julia said. "They built it from the ground up, right in Wilton."

After several more shots of the business, we proceeded to the family home, a sprawling ranch house in the woods outside Wilton. Dad posing next to his four-wheel-drive pickup truck. Mom next to her Ford station wagon. A Jesus Is Lord sticker adorned the bumper. Dad posing with various dead fish, deer, and fowl. Mom working on quilts and afghans.

"You're an only child?"

"Yep," Julia said. "I was a miracle baby. Mom had a lot of female problems, as they say. Anyway, they didn't think she'd be able to give birth. But here I am."

The parade of photos continued with shots of Julia's baptism.

Young Julia, soaking wet, looked absolutely darling in her white robe. "Oh, you were so cute," I said. *Don't start talking about her looks.* "How old were you?"

"Ten," she said.

"What denomination?" I said.

"One hundred percent Southern Baptist. Dad's a deacon. Mom's a Sunday school teacher. I never had a chance. They don't know I've stopped going to church."

"Eeek," I said. "I was raised that way too. It's hard to break away."

"I can't face any more screaming sermons. I can't believe in the black-and-white Baptist universe."

"I know what you mean."

Eventually, new faces appeared. Grandparents, great aunts, great uncles, cousins, uncles, aunts. We reached a section with several shots of a pair of tow-headed girls.

"Is that you?" I said.

"Yeah, me and my cousin Louanne. We played together all the time when we were growing up. We were like sisters. During the summers, we spent every day together up until we were twelve or thirteen. People used to mistake us for twins."

"Where is she now?"

"Oh, she's here in town at LTU. She's a resident assistant in one of the dorms."

"You don't say?" I wondered whether Louanne could help me get in touch with Rachel Metcalf, the preacher's daughter.

"Yeah, her whole family are big-time holy rollers. Louanne was destined to go to LTU from birth."

"Are you on speaking terms with her?"

"Of course." Giving me a puzzled look, Julia closed the photo album and stood up.

"I need some information about an LTU student. I'd really like to meet Rachel Metcalf. Do you think Louanne could help?"

"What's all this about?"

"Do you know anything about the murder of Rebecca Metcalf?"

"Yeah, I think I've heard something about it. What about it?"

I gave Julia a rundown of what I'd learned.

"I don't think Louanne would want to get involved," she said firmly.

"You don't have to tell her the whole story."

"I can't lie to her. She's family. Besides, she might get in trouble." Her green eyes growing angry, Julia had started to pace around the small room.

"No she won't." I tried to sound reassuring.

"How do you know? That school is practically like a prison, with all the snitching and security. Any violation of rules is supposed to be reported to school authorities. Even chaplains have to snitch on code violators. There's an eleven p.m. curfew for women. Mandatory chapel twice a week. Dress codes. They keep strict tabs on everybody. I can't drag her into this."

She was right. It was too much to ask. "Never mind. I'm sorry I brought it up."

"She likes it out there. I don't want her to get in trouble."

"Forget I said anything."

"You can be expelled from that school just for drinking."

"Just drop it."

Julia paused. "Listen, I can call and ask. But I won't pressure her."

"I couldn't ask for more than that," I said. I was smiling. "Thanks."

She sat back down on the bed. We stayed there a while without looking at each other.

"Well, what do you want to do now?" Julia said.

"I don't care."

"Want to watch TV?"

"I don't know. Whatever you want to do."

"I could make some popcorn."

"I'm not really hungry," I said. "Look, maybe I should take off. It's getting late, and I'm sure you have things to do."

"No, really. I like having you hang out, if you don't mind." Julia leaned back against wall. Her Hawaiian shirt was open, exposing much of her tank top. She was braless again tonight.

I liked hanging out all right. Too much for my own good.

"If you want to go, that's all right too."

I stood up. The tension was driving me crazy. I might have screamed if I had sat next to her any longer.

"Carmen?"

"What?" I said.

"What's wrong?"

"Just jumpy, I guess." Ready to jump out of my skin.

"Listen, you don't have to humor me. If you want to go, just go."

I looked at her. She smiled at me with her beautiful green eyes. My pulse racing, I cleared my throat. "Being here is just kind of hard for me."

Julia looked hurt. "What am I doing wrong?"

"Nothing," I said.

"Don't you like me?"

I paused. "Julia, don't you get it? Of course I like you. That's the problem. I like you so much that being around you is tough for me."

"What do you mean?" Julia said.

"I'm attracted to you. Can't you tell? I mean, you really get to me. I didn't want to feel this way about you. I never wanted to feel this way again about anybody. But here I am, making a fool out of myself."

"You're not making a fool of yourself," she said. She sat up and folded her arms over her chest. There was a long pause. "I am truly flattered that you are attracted to me."

"Jesus Christ," I said. She was going to hit me with the speech. "Spare me. I've heard this before."

"Look, you're not the only one feeling things here," she said. Taking a long breath, she rubbed her hands nervously over the legs of her long, baggy shorts. "I feel things for you, too. Things I'm not sure of yet. But I like to be around you. I can't even believe I'm telling you this. It scares me."

88

"I'm not going to leap on you."

Julia looked at the wall. "Look, Carmen, I'm confused right now. I've had sex with one man. To tell you the truth, it wasn't all that great. Have you ever had sex with a man?"

"No. I never wanted to."

"I wasn't really attracted to him, but he was so gung-ho about it, I figured why not give it a whirl? I guess that makes me stupid."

"You don't have to explain yourself to me."

She paused again. "When I was growing up, I never had strong feelings for boys, but I thought that was because I was a good girl. I always took the church so seriously. Well, anyway, I always enjoyed the company of other girls. I felt strongly about them. Admired their beauty, their character. I guess you could say I had crushes on them."

She's telling you the big lavender secret. "Oh God," I said. My nerves were going to be permanently shot after this evening.

"Anyway, what I'm trying to say is that I like you too. I mean, I admire you. I think you're very beautiful. And I don't know what that means yet. But I'd like to go out with you. I mean, I'd like to date you. I don't know about the other stuff yet. But I really think you're an exciting, attractive woman. She looked small and confused sitting there on the bed. And very beautiful.

I sat next to her.

"Can I put my arm around you?" I said.

"Yes," she said, tentatively.

Slowly and carefully, I slipped my arm around her shoulder. "Julia, you're safe with me. I'm not out to take advantage of you. I would be honored to go out with you, to get to know you better."

"You are so sweet," she said.

I felt embarrassed that she thought so. "Thanks," I said. "Look, I'm going to go now. I think we should think this through. I don't want to rush anything."

"You're probably right."

I walked to the door.

"Let me walk you to your car."

We walked to the Civic without speaking. I unlocked the door.

Julia looked at me. "I wish you didn't have to go."

"My grandmother keeps really close tabs on me. She'd be worried sick if I didn't show up."

"You're a grownup."

"That's what you think," I said. I glanced around. The campus seemed deserted. Let the hidden homophobes out prowling late at night be damned. "Can I give you a hug?"

"Please," Julia said.

I had intended a quick embrace, but she held me tightly. Every part of my body felt alive and connected to hers. After a long while, we separated.

"Thanks," I said.

"Thank *you*."

"Are you all right?"

"Sure," she said.

I kissed her hand. "You take care now. I gotta go," I said. I waited until she was safe in the building, and then I drove off, happier than I had been in my entire life.

* * * * *

As soon as I got home, I realized my happiness would be fleeting. I saw my psychic grandmother peering out the back door at me as I got out of the Civic. I knew there would be hell to pay. I had new motivation to find a different place to live.

The next morning, I phoned Raúl at the travel agency.

"This is Carmen."

"What is the matter?"

"I need a loan." It was the first time I had ever asked him for money.

"Is something wrong?"

"My living arrangements aren't working out very well. I need to find a new place, and I don't have time to save up for deposits."

"I see," he said. "Of course I'll be glad to help."

"Thanks," I said.

"I know you must be desperate to ask. You never want my help. Do you want to tell me about it?"

"It's Grandma. You know how she is. But you can be sure I'll pay back every penny with interest."

"I know you will, Carmen," he said.

It was time for a war council with Grandma. I braced myself and headed over to her house.

I walked in the back door and found her sitting in her recliner and watching *As the World Turns*.

"Hi, Grandma," I said.

When she refused to look away from the TV, I turned it off.

"What do you think you're doing?"

"We gotta talk, old girl."

She glowered at me and lit up a cigar. Shit, she was resorting to chemical warfare.

"Make it quick," she said. "I don't want to miss my show."

"Grandma, I love you dearly, but we can't live like this anymore. You don't like what I'm up to half the time, and I don't like the feeling you're always watching me. I don't think it's healthy."

She puffed at her cigar. "Healthy? What the hell do you know about healthy? You do what you want. I ain't got no hold on you."

"Right," I said. "You silly old goat. You're the only mother I've ever known. Of course you have a hold on me."

The old woman started crying.

"Please don't make this out like I'm stabbing you in the back. I'm nearly twenty-five years old. It's time for me to move along."

She continued bawling. "It's some gal, ain't it? You gonna shack up with one of those perverts again?"

"I am seeing someone — on a friendly basis," I said. But I'm moving out on my own."

She let out a long, low moan. "I knew it. I knew it."

"I know you did."

She stubbed out her cigar violently. "Well, this time, when she dumps you flat, you ain't crawling back here. You hear me? You ain't tearing up my life again. I ain't running no freak show. You pack up and get out. And don't you think you can bring your sicko friends over here either. This is my house."

"I know it is, Grandma." I turned away.

"Do you know what the Bible says about your lifestyle? Says it's an abomination. Says you're going to burn in hell. That's God talking. Not me. Lord knows, I tried to raise you right. I should have never let you stop going to church."

"Grandma," I said, "I would not go back to the Baptist Church if you had a gun to my head. Do you understand? I'll never go back. Ever. And if you think I'm going to burn in hell for the way I am, then so be it."

"The Bible says there will be mockers in the last time, who will walk after their own ungodly lusts."

"Stop. Please."

"Look it up if you don't believe me. It's in Jude."

"I've read the Bible."

"The devils in hell can quote the scriptures."

"I am not a devil. I am just a lesbian."

"First it was your mother and that low-down Porta-Rican. Might as well have been a nigger, he was so black. And now you, turning out like some kind of freak. I don't know why I deserve this."

As I walked out, I felt tears streaming down my face. I wished she had beaten me. It would have hurt less.

CHAPTER 5

By the middle of the week, I had placed a deposit on a small garage apartment near FCU — thanks to Raúl's check. The neighborhood wasn't great, but the rent was cheap. My landlords — the Brauns — were an older married couple. They were nervous about the cats and insisted that I give them a deposit for any damage the cats might wreak in the apartment — in addition to rent security. They said I could move in whenever I wanted to. I hoped they wouldn't be too nosy. The place was about the same size as Grandma's and I figured I could fix it up just as nicely.

I spent the mornings and nights packing. I didn't own much, and I was able to make a lot of progress. As I came and went, I saw Grandma peering out her back window at me. I knew she would never take back what she had said, although she probably regretted it.

Early Wednesday morning, I set out for my appointment with Principal Hawkins. I was dressed in my oft-worn navy suit. If I were to continue this detective business, I would have to invest in some new dress clothes. I arrived at the school about ten minutes early. Mrs. Jenkins, the school secretary, an evil-looking woman with badly dyed red hair, eyed me disdainfully as I approached the dark wooden barricade dividing the school's inner sanctum from the rest of the world.

"I'm here to see Dr. Hawkins," I said.

"Do you have an appointment?"

"Yes. I'm Carla Sullivan."

She took her time as she looked over her desk calendar. Finally, she opened the swinging door that divided the outer and inner offices. "The principal will see you in a moment," she said as she ushered me in.

Hawkins' office was just as depressing as any principal's office I had ever been sent to during my tumultuous school career. I reminded myself that I was an adult, and that the principal could neither give me swats nor add harmful information to my permanent record.

Her desk was gun-metal gray, the chairs institutional blond. I scanned her office for signs of humanity. Her shelves were lined with books on school administration and child psychology. Various framed degrees hung on the walls — her doctorate in education was most prominent — and on her desk was a framed photo of a self-satisfied looking balding man, her husband, I guessed. As I waited, the clock — the kind found only in public schools, psychiatric wards, and prisons — ticked off the minutes with a heavy thud. I was ready to either walk out or scream when at last the good doctor appeared, dressed in a dark blue business suit, a compact woman in her mid-forties, with graying, dark brown hair — arranged neatly in a short permed coif. Her eyes were blue and commanding.

"Miss Sullivan, I presume," she said.

I paused. I had to get much smoother at this alias business. "Yes," I said, rising to shake her hand.

She pumped my hand once — stiffly. "Please, sit down." I returned to my chair.

"I must admit, I have never seen your byline in the *Herald*. My husband and I subscribe to both city papers. We like to stay on top of things."

The comment knocked me off balance. "Is your husband also in the education field?" I said.

"Oh, heavens no. One pauper in the family is quite enough, I should say."

"Indeed."

"Mr. Hawkins is in the oil business, which can be

far more lucrative, but is also extremely volatile, I must say."

I felt like gagging. This woman referred to her own husband as Mr. Hawkins. What did she call him in the sack — Mr. Stud?

"Well, I won't waste any more of your time, Dr. Hawkins. I know you have your hands full running this school."

"That's for certain," she said.

"Let me just ask you a few questions about Diane and Rebecca."

"A very sad topic indeed, but the press can't seem to get its fill."

"Were there ever any indications that Rebecca was a victim of sexual abuse?"

The principal inhaled thoughtfully. "I'm sure you're aware, Miss Sullivan, that school personnel are required to report all suspected cases of child abuse. We saw no such evidence."

"Were there any . . . behavior problems?"

She gave me a condescending look. "Nothing that stands out in my mind. We very rarely see children who behave as angels in our school. Growing up is a time of testing boundaries. We see that from most of our children."

"So nothing about Rebecca's behavior stood out?"

"As I have just said."

"Was there anybody at the school who was interested in Diane sexually? A spurned suitor, perhaps?"

"Not that I was aware of."

"Any odd relationships or tensions that perhaps you had a hunch about?"

"I'm afraid not."

I paused. "Did you see anything abnormal about Diane?"

"As I have told the press before, she was a perfectly competent teacher. I had no reason to suspect any abnormal behavior."

"What kind of person was she?"

"I beg your pardon?"

"What kind of impression did you draw of her character? Was she a solid citizen? Warm-hearted? Friendly? Reliable?"

"As I have said, Miss Sullivan, Miss Barrett was a competent, dedicated teacher. I know little about her private life." Hawkins' face remained impassive.

"But you worked with her for many years."

"My teachers' lives are their own. I do not pry into them."

"I see," I said. "Do you think Diane was capable of molesting and murdering Rebecca Metcalf?"

"My business is not law enforcement, Miss Sullivan. I believe in the system."

I sighed. Myra Hawkins was as slick as a presidential press secretary fending off questions at a press conference. She could have stood up to torture from the KGB without cracking. "Well, thank you for your time. I guess that's all I needed to know."

Profoundly dissatisfied, I left her office.

Thursday morning, I got ready for my meeting with the Reverend Metcalf. Wearing the same old pantsuit, I pulled up outside the large octagonal church ten minutes early for my ten-thirty appointment. His study, I was told by his secretary, was in the west wing.

I followed the signs and found the church secretary's office, which was bigger than the pastors office at my old church and contained deep gold carpeting and walnut paneling. The secretary was a cheerful woman in her mid-thirties.

"What can I do for you?" she said.

"I have an appointment with Rev. Metcalf."

"Carla?"

"Yes."

"Well, have a seat. He'll be with you in a moment."

I sat down on the huge leather sofa in her office and watched her work at an IBM computer that looked brand new. The rest of the office equipment was state-of-the-art: a gleaming AT&T console telephone and two Xerox photocopy machines with built-in collators. This church was obviously loaded, unlike my old one, which used outmoded equipment it picked up at auctions or from donations.

Metcalf, tall and commanding, walked out of his study. "Carla, come on in," he said in a soft, concerned voice. His office was mammoth enough to serve the CEO of a major corporation. A huge, antique rolltop desk overlooking a picture window sat against the wall. It was flanked by two bookcases full of religious writings. I sat on the sumptuous leather sofa while Metcalf sat at the leather chair near his desk.

"This is quite a set-up you have here," I said.

"In John 10:10, Jesus said, 'I have come that they might have life, and that they might have it more abundantly.' What you see here is abundant living."

If I had been in an argumentative mood, I could have hit him with: "It is easier for a camel to go through the eye of a needle than for a rich man to enter the kingdom of God." But I merely nodded at him.

"So what is your need today?" he said earnestly. "Lay it at the foot of the cross. We serve a mighty God. The Bible says, 'We have not because we ask not.' "

"Reverend, I'm a journalist."

"Yes, "he said. "And what organization do you represent?"

"The *Herald.*"

"I see. And what is this about?"

I was on the verge of losing my nerve. "I am investigating your daughter's death. I think the wrong person was blamed for the murder."

For a moment, he looked angry and flustered, but his composure returned quickly. "My sovereign Lord Jesus Christ took Rebecca home with him. That's all I know about her passing."

"Do you think Diane Barrett killed her?"

"I leave that in the hands of the Lord," he said calmly.

"I see," I said. I was feeling sheepish and stupid.

"Is that all you wanted to know?"

"No. There's something else — about your wife."

"Yes?"

"According to news accounts, LaDonna Metcalf ran off the road six months before her death. Were drugs or alcohol involved?"

His face turned stormy again. Was it indignation or grief that swept over him? Just as quickly, he grew calm again. "No charges were ever filed against my wife," he said in a measured voice.

"Was she depressed or suicidal?"

He looked astonished. "What possible news value could that have to your readers, Miss Sullivan?"

I was at a loss to tell him. "And what was the cause of her death?"

"She was ill. The Lord took her home," he said. His expression was steely, but his voice remained calm.

"In retrospect, did you ever suspect that somebody had tried to molest Rebecca? A neighbor or baby sitter perhaps?"

"Miss Sullivan, if I had thought that somebody was hurting my daughter, I would have done everything in my power to protect her." His expression grew distressed.

I didn't have the nerve to grill him further. "Thank you, Reverend, for your cooperation," I said.

He stood up and showed me to the door. "I trust you won't approach Rachel with any of these questions. Her mental health is very precarious," he said, his voice emphatic.

I nodded at him but did not answer.

Sunday was moving day. I had rented a truck for the day. Julia walked over early that morning to help. We were nearly finished loading when Grandma returned from church.

"Who is this?" Grandma demanded.

"Grandma, this is my friend Julia Nichols. Julia this is my grandmother, Mrs. Edna Sullivan."

"You were just gonna take off without telling me?" the old woman said.

"Of course not," I said.

She scowled at Julia and said to me: "You moving in with her?"

"No, I have a place that's not far from here. I left you a note on the counter. It has my new address. My phone number will be the same as it is now."

"Your daddy paying for this?"

"He's helping."

Grandma opened her jeweled straw purse and removed her wallet. "Here's some money. Take care of yourself."

She handed me two hundred and fifty dollars and then walked into the house. I followed her into the kitchen.

"I can't take this money."

"Yes you can."

"It's yours. I want to be on my own now."

"You keep it. Now you get on outta here. I've done the best I can for you."

"I know you have. Thank you."

She hugged me, and we both cried for a long time.

"Listen, I've cleaned the place out," I said, wiping away my tears. "The floors, windows, and fixtures are all sparkling."

"Who's your new landlord?"

"Mr. and Mrs. Karl Braun."

"How's that last name spelled?"

"B-R-A-U-N." I knew what was coming next.

"You know, Hitler's mistress was named Braun. I wonder if they're related. Bunch of filthy German Nazi bastards. I never knew why we dropped the A-bomb on the Japs and not on them."

I knew better than to argue.

"Well," she said, "don't keep your gal waiting."

"Thanks again for the money," I said.

As I was walking away, she said: "Don't forget to come by and pick some vegetables. I don't want the damn things to spoil."

Late that night, Julia and I — hot, grimy, and exhausted — sat amid boxes as the cats bounced around the new apartment. We had both been shy around each other all week at work, and that day we had been too preoccupied with hauling boxes to think about what we had started just a week ago.

"I can't thank you enough for your help. You want me to drive you home now?" I asked. "It's nearly midnight."

"No," she said.

"Well, I don't think I can unpack another box. If I don't go now, I'm afraid I'll pass out. And it's too dangerous for you to walk."

"What if I just stayed here?" she said.

My heart began to pound. She wanted to stay here? "Here?"

"We're both exhausted. I'm ready to fall asleep now."

"Here?" I said.

"If you don't want me to stay, that's okay," she said.

"No, Julia. Of course you're welcome."

She'd said "here," but she probably didn't mean *here*. I opened the box marked sheets and towels and started making up the couch.

"You don't have to do that," Julia said.

"Well, you can take the bed," I said.

"I thought I'd just crawl in with you, if that's okay."

This can't be. It's happening too fast. "Are you sure?"

"Carmen, I thought about you all week. I'm sure."

Julia followed me to the bathroom. I handed her a fresh bar of soap, toothbrush, and a towel.

In a little while, she emerged, wearing only the towel. The sight of so much Julia took my breath away. I looked at the floor.

"I think you'll be comfortable in these," I said, handing her a clean T-shirt and panties as I averted my eyes. I quickly headed to the bathroom.

By the time I got out of the shower, Julia had fallen asleep. She looked beautiful and childlike. I turned out the lights and quietly slipped in bed, my pulse racing frantically. *Be very careful not to touch her.*

"Carmen?"

"Yeah."

"I fell asleep."

"I noticed."

"You want to hold me?" Julia said.

"Yeah," I said, "but I'm scared."

"Me too."

I scooted away from the edge of the bed. Slipping up against her back, I placed my arm around her waist. My whole body was tingling.

"Is this okay?" I said.

"It was just what I needed. Thanks," she said.

"Thank *you*," I said.

Before I knew it, I was fast asleep.

The next morning, I woke up, surprised to find Julia sleeping in my bed. Trying to be as quiet as possible, I got up and started some coffee. Julia sat up in bed as soon as the coffee maker started wheezing.

"Hi," she said. She looked beautiful and tousled. Yawning languidly, she stretched and then ruffled her blonde hair.

"Good morning. I'm making some coffee."

"I heard."

"Are you in a hurry to get back to campus?"

"I can stay a while."

We had coffee and toasted English muffins.

"This is great strawberry jam," Julia said.

"Grandma sure is a terror when it comes to making jams and pickles. She goes down to Stilwell every year to get the best strawberries," I said. Suddenly, I was filled with worry about the old woman. "I just hope she's okay."

"Carmen, you're twenty-four. It's time to be on your own."

"I know," I said. "But she's lost a lot of people in her life. My Uncle Buster in a hunting accident back when he was in high school, Grandpa to a heart attack, then my mom. That's why she holds onto me so tightly. I felt tears rolling down my cheeks.

"You're going to make it," Julia said. "And so is she."

"Sorry," I said. "I don't mean to put you through all this angst."

"It's all right. I care about you."

"I don't know what to make of all this, Julia."

"All this what?"

"You and me, spending so much time together, sleeping in the same bed."

"Don't worry so much."

"That's like telling a bee not to buzz," I said. I looked at her and longed to hold her.

"What are you thinking about?" she asked.

"You don't want to know."

"Why? Does my hair look funny?"

"No," I said.

"Then what?"

"I want you."

"Know what?"

"What?"

"I want you too."

My heart took off at a Kentucky Derby gallop. "What'll we do now?" I said.

"You're the one with experience."

I looked at her and I knew I was in love. "Look, I'm scared to death right now. I went through a very difficult breakup about a year ago, and I'm still pretty fragile emotionally. I have to protect myself now. If this isn't serious for you, now's the time to let me know."

"Carmen, I am serious."

"I have to know that this isn't just some kind of

experiment for you. I mean, I have to know that you care about me."

"Of course I do."

"You mean it?"

"Yes. I mean it."

I stuck out my hand and led Julia to the couch. We sat down together.

"You don't have to do anything you don't want to," I said. "Just let me know if anything feels weird."

"I will," Julia said.

I began kissing her on the cheek and gently brushing my face against hers. She was soft. So soft. And then, Julia turned her mouth toward mine and kissed me. Suddenly, my whole body was ignited with passion radiating from that tender kiss. But I had to wait for her, to let her set the pace. Her mouth lingered. And lingered. We drew closer, wrapping our arms around each other. Soon, her tongue was plunging into my mouth. We kissed like that for a long time.

I kissed her neck, and Julia began moaning softly. My body was racing with passion.

Leaning back, she lifted up her T-shirt and guided my hands toward her breasts. She held me as I lay on top of her. I gently touched her soft, white flesh and lightly brushed her tender pink nipples. I kissed her between her breasts. And then my mouth found her nipple.

I paused. She pulled my mouth against her. I kissed her gently and slowly, and she began writhing against me. My mouth explored her belly and moved down. Eventually, I reached her panty line. Her breathing grew heavier, and so did mine. I could smell the scent. Sweet, wonderful, overwhelming. It drew me.

She slid off the panties and lay back down in front of me. Very carefully, I brushed her blonde hair. She gasped. There was no need to hurry.

"We can stop."

"Don't stop," she said.

She spread her legs slightly, and my finger dipped between the lips. Again, she gasped. She was incredibly wet. I gently stroked her as I kissed her belly, my mouth careful not to stray too low.

"I'll do anything you want," I said.

"Please. Please."

It was all I needed to hear.

The next time I was aware of time, it was past noon, and we were still lying together on the couch.

"Are you all right?" I said.

"I'll say."

"Julia, my dearest, I don't want to scare you off, but I'm in love with you."

She kissed me lightly on the cheek. "I'm not scared. I love you too."

"Does this mean we're going steady?"

"I guess so," she said with a laugh. "Hey, isn't it your turn yet?"

"Are you sure you want to?"

"After all that? Of course."

"Honey, I don't want to rush you. Don't feel obligated."

"It isn't exactly obligation that I'm feeling, Carmen. I think lust would be a more appropriate term."

I laughed. "You're the boss."

I let Julia take over. She was a natural.

That week, Julia and I spent a lot of time getting acquainted and setting up the new apartment. Wiley had instantly accepted Julia as a member of the family. Holly was standoffish, but soon he was following her around, rubbing her legs, and shamelessly planting himself on her lap whenever she sat down.

I phoned Grandma two or three times a day to remind her that I was nearby if she had a problem. After several days of this, she told me to stop pestering her and come over and mow her lawn if I was so worried about her. I did so the next morning.

The Barrett matter was never far from my mind. Julia finally called her cousin Louanne to arrange for me to meet Rachel Metcalf. I took a bubble bath while she chatted with Louanne on the phone. My new apartment had a huge claw-footed tub that was big enough for me, at five-foot-six, to float in. Finally, Julia appeared in the doorway. "She says she can smuggle us in during visitors weekend."

"Was she difficult to persuade?"

Julia sighed. "I had to threaten to tell Aunt Mavis that I had seen her smoke a cigarette when she was nine years old."

"Will she ever forgive you?"

"I doubt it, Carmen. She can't even forgive herself for one cigarette. She's Pentecostal."

"What do we have to do?"

"Well, the campus is going to be filled with religious fanatic high school kids. They open the campus once a month for visits."

"How do we get to Rachel?"

"That, Louanne said, is our problem," Julia said. "She also said we would be subject to all campus rules. That includes mandatory skirts for women in chapel and class. She said that we would be thrown out at the slightest hint of trouble."

"I haven't had a skirt on in years. I'll have to shave my legs. And I suppose necking with you would be out of the question?"

"I think the Apostle Paul would have something to say about the necking. Detective work carries a high price," she said.

"I suppose," I said. "We have to work out a cover story. What would make a twenty-four-year-old woman consider attending Lovell Taft University?"

"A sudden conversion?"

"I don't want to get struck dead for blasphemy. I'll just say I've been working as a typist since graduation, and I'm eager to attend college to improve my chances for landing a better job. Lovell is into the prosperity Gospel. That will fit in just fine out here. So what about you?"

"I think I'll just keep it simple. I'll tell them I'm considering transferring to LTU. I'll tell them I'm sick of the sinful, secular atmosphere."

"That's good. Just don't overdo the sinful, secular bit."

"You're the one with the false name and made-up life story, Carmen."

"I have to protect my job. If anybody finds out about this, I could be fired."

"I think you just enjoy the intrigue."

I threw a handful of sudsy water at her.

"We'll see about that," she said. She walked to the sink, filled a cup with cold water, and dumped it on my head.

"No fair," I said, but she ran out of the room before I could retaliate.

CHAPTER 6

Although I was still in Sargent's doghouse, he agreed to let me take off Friday and Saturday and make up the days later.

Friday afternoon, Julia and I went to a thrift shop, where I picked up a couple of cotton skirts. Back in my new apartment, Julia and I packed. Julia lent me a couple of her dresses and blouses. I packed hair spray and my seldom-used makeup kit. Then, I pondered the unthinkable.

I headed toward the bathroom with my Gillette

foamy and Bic razor. "I wish I were in Europe. Then I wouldn't have to do this. I had a professor who claimed that in France, only the prostitutes shave their legs."

I sat on the edge of the tub and lathered up my calves. "You know, no matter what I do, I'm still going to stick out like a lesbian truck driver at the debutante ball."

Julia stood in the doorway and laughed. "Now I can take you home to meet mother, honey pie."

It was a beautiful day for driving, even if we were headed to LTU. The sky was crystal blue, a few white puffy clouds floated in the distance, the air was pleasantly warm, without being oppressive. We headed west on the expressway. The Arkansas was ruddy and sluggish that day, but the smell from the petroleum refineries wasn't bad; the wind was blowing the other way. As we went farther south, the lawns got bigger and the houses farther back from the road. Soon, we were within sight of the campus, the giant golden praying hands atop Taft's prayer center gleaming in the distance.

The campus was arrestingly modern — everything built out of shiny golden glass and steel, not a scrap of ivy to be found anywhere. Irreverent locals called the South Side landmark by some less-than-flattering names — Six Flags Over Jesus, Taft's Tinkertoy Village, and Lovell's Folly.

"You didn't tell Louanne about us, did you?" I asked, as we walked toward Maranatha Hall, the dormitory where Louanne lived. I was wearing dress slacks, loafers, and an oxford shirt. My legs were still smarting from their ordeal.

"Of course I did," Julia replied. "I really want to spend the entire weekend having demons cast out of me."

A perky blonde in a red LTU sweat suit greeted us at the door. "Froggie!" she screamed at Julia.

"Toad!" replied Julia. The two embraced and giggled. I stood holding my suitcase.

When the squealing finally died down, Julia turned to me: "Carmen, this is my cousin Louanne. Louanne, this is my good friend Carmen."

"Pleased to meet you," I said. I offered my hand, which she shook stiffly. She hated me.

"Likewise," Louanne said.

"As you know, I'm a journalist, so I'm going to ask you to call me Carla. It's important that I keep my identity secret."

"I just hope you're not out to destroy this ministry. God has ordained Brother Lovell and this ministry to bring healing to this generation."

"Believe me, I would never set out to do battle with God," I said with a laugh. "The Almighty and I are close, personal friends."

Louanne looked at me humorlessly. "I hope you're serious about being a friend of God," she said. "Galatians 6:7 tells us: 'Be not deceived, God is not mocked, for whatever a man soweth, that shall he also reap.' "

Julia broke in: "Why don't we go inside and get set up?"

"Fine," Louanne said. She led us to her room.

As a resident assistant, her single was large by

dormitory standards. Louanne had set up two army cots for our stay. I scanned the room, which was adorned with a multitude of religious plaques, posters, and samplers. Everywhere I turned, there was a scripture verse to catch the eye or a rendering of Jesus healing a cripple, cradling a sheep, or walking on water.

Louanne's voice shook me from my contemplation. "Fill these out and wear them at all our gatherings." She handed us name tags. "Well, I'll let you two get settled. I have to go back downstairs to help visitors check in."

"Go right ahead," Julia said.

Louanne paused at the door. "You both know this is a Christian university. I trust that you understand the rules. She turned and walked out."

"I don't know how much of this I can stand," I said.

Julia shook her head and sat on the bed. "This was your idea, Carmen. Surely you can last a few hours."

I shrugged. "What was the froggie bit?"

"When we were little, Aunt Mavis or my mom would put us out in a little baby pool, and we would just sit there for hours, splashing and laughing and having a good time. That's where we got the names. We loved the water."

"I see," I said. "By the way, what's Louanne's major?"

"Ministry, with a specialization in New Testament studies."

"Saints preserve us," I said.

* * * * *

Later that evening, the women of Maranatha Hall's second floor and their visitors — about thirty in all — gathered in a common room for what had been billed as a session of sharing. Each toted a Bible. By the time Julia and I got to the room, most of the seats were taken, so we sat near the door. I wore an Indian print blue cotton skirt, huaraches, and a blue cotton blouse. I looked a lot more like a hippy Earth Mother than a holy roller, but I hadn't had time to order from the Phyllis Schlafly "Dress for Subjugation" catalogue. I spotted Rachel Metcalf across the room. She was a small woman, about five-foot-two, with pale skin and delicate features, smoky gray eyes, and auburn hair.

Louanne, as floor resident assistant and lay chaplain, led the meeting.

"Hi, I'm Louanne."

"Hi, Louanne," the room echoed.

"Tonight, good sisters in Christ, I'm going to share a scripture verse with you, and I'd like all of you to talk about what it means in your life."

"Amen," the women in the room replied.

Great. I was trapped again, and this time, it was worse than the Tabernacle of Hope. I wasn't going to be able to cough my way out of this prayer meeting.

"Tonight, my dear sisters, our text will be Luke 18:16. But first let's open with a word of prayer."

Heads around the room bowed in obedience. Everyone in the room joined hands. I lowered my head, but kept my eyes open. I couldn't see Rachel, whom I had spotted straight across the room from me.

"Father in Heaven," Louanne said earnestly, "You promised us that when two or three of us are gathered in Your name, You would be present among us. Well, tonight, we are gathered in Your name, and we know You are here among us."

Several more amens rose from the room. Some of the people around me were swaying. The room was cool, but I was sweating as if I were in a sauna. Julia clutched my hand for dear life.

"Father, You gave us Your Word as a sign of Your presence among us."

A woman near me muttered, "Yes, Lord."

"Father, we ask that as we break open Your Word, this Bread of Life, that You fill us with Your precious wisdom and that You open our hearts to Your grace and love."

From across the room, I heard someone moan: "Sweet Jesus."

"We ask this in the name of Jesus Christ, Your holy begotten son, through whom all good things come. Amen."

The room erupted in a chorus of amens and thank-you Lords.

As we raised our heads, Louanne, beaming, said: "Isn't life sweet with the Lord?"

Her flock nodded in agreement. What was wrong with these people? Why didn't we all just run for the door?

"Our text is Luke 18:16," she said. Pages rattled as the women searched for the scripture.

Louanne turned to me. "Carla, would you like to introduce yourself and read our scripture verse?"

"Who me?" I said, in panic. She really hated me. A lot.

"Yes, please."

I clutched my name tag. "Hi. I'm Carla."

"Hi, Carla," the women replied.

I cleared my throat. "Luke 18:16: 'Suffer little children to come unto me, and forbid them not; for of such is the kingdom of God.' "

"Thank you, sister," Louanne said. "Let's begin with the sharing."

I was relieved when Louanne started the process, thus ending my speaking duties. She recounted numerous times throughout her life in which she came to the Lord with the simplicity of a child and was rewarded with miracles large and small. Throughout Louanne's account, I stole occasional glances at Rachel, who had a strange, vacant look on her face.

Various residents expounded on the meaning of that verse in their lives. One upbeat redhead named Rhonda talked about how, after a life of sin and degradation, she had given her heart to Jesus at age eleven.

At that point I nearly screamed, but I reminded myself that I was surrounded and outnumbered.

As the meeting wore on, it became apparent that all the floor residents were expected to speak. Finally, it was Rachel's turn.

"Rachel, would you like to say anything?" Louanne asked.

Rachel's face turned deep red. "What should I say?"

"Anything that's on your heart that you think would help minister to our guests," Louanne replied.

Her face contorted in anger. "I can't talk about this," she said. "I wish I knew why children had to suffer if Jesus loves them so much." She began weeping.

Louanne stood up. "Rachel, the Lord has laid all this on your heart to bring you to greater perfection in Him. Your sisters in Christ are going to pray you through this. We love you. Prayer warriors, please rise."

I looked around me for women in armor. Four ordinary-looking women stood up and approached Louanne.

"Please surround your sister in the love of Christ," Louanne ordered.

The women surrounded Rachel and embraced her. She disappeared under the huddle.

What the hell were they doing to her? I looked at Julia. She looked back, equally confused. Some of the young visitors also seemed bewildered. But among the residents, there was calm. Perhaps this sort of hubbub was commonplace, what with Louanne running the show.

"Let us pray," Louanne ordered.

Everyone except for me and Julia bowed their heads in prayer. In a loud, commanding voice, Louanne said: "Lord, You promised that when two or more of us agree in prayer, our Father in Heaven will do what we ask. Lord, we are in agreement tonight."

"Yes, yes," said the prayer warrior huddle.

"Lord Jesus, we pray that a spirit of peace come over our sister Rachel. We want that peace that passes all understanding."

"Amen," the huddle replied.

Around me, I heard jumbled, sing-song speech. They were praying in tongues again. My heart raced with panic, but I couldn't leave. I had see what would happen to Rachel.

"The Prophet Isaiah tells us: You were wounded for our transgressions. You were bruised for our iniquities. Surely You bore our sorrows. And with Your stripes we are healed."

"Oh yes, oh yes," the huddle replied.

"Jesus, by the power of Your stripes, we pray that You lift the burden of sorrow from our sister Rachel. Free her, Lord Jesus. Free her now," Louanne said in a booming voice that frightened me deeply.

"Free her, free her," the huddle repeated.

It seemed to be some sort of exorcism.

"We tell the spirits of doubt and despair to be gone in the mighty name of Jesus."

"Be gone, be gone," came the reply.

This definitely was some sort of exorcism.

"Thou foul spirits, loose this servant of Christ, in the mighty name of Jesus," Louanne commanded. Her face was fierce and wild. "Satan, we bind you by the blood of Christ."

Then Louanne said, her voice soft again, "Let her up, warriors."

The huddle backed away, and women returned to their seats.

Thank God. Maybe they would leave her alone now.

"Rachel, stand up, and praise God, and claim your miracle in the name of Jesus," Louanne ordered.

Rachel, stunned and disoriented, remained seated.

"Use your prayer language," Louanne said.

Rachel said nothing. Her eyes were not focused.

Enough was enough. "Something's gone wrong with her," I whispered. "We've got to do something."

Julia nodded. Mastering my panic, I stood up and tapped Louanne on the shoulder. "I need to speak to you outside," I whispered.

"Quench not the Spirit of God," Louanne replied.

I looked around the room. I was afraid the prayer warriors would leap on me. But there was no sign of action from them or the rest of the crowd.

"Come with us, Louanne," Julia said gently.

Reluctantly, she followed us into the hall.

"I think somebody should take Rachel to the hospital," I said. "I'm no psychiatrist, but something's wrong with that woman in there. She's catatonic or psychotic or something."

"God can cure anything," Louanne said, her face flushed, her eyes steely and determined. "Greater is He that is in me than He that is in the world."

Louanne was really getting on my nerves with that machine-gun Bible mouth of hers. Maybe I should have smacked her a good one over the head with a deluxe, leather-bound, family-size Scofield chain-reference Bible. "We have to get help," I said. "God works through doctors, too."

"She's had doctors and hospitals for years," Louanne said. "They didn't help her. We're trying to pray her through this."

"I know you're trying to help," I said, "but I don't think she can stand up to any more of this right now. She needs a chance to recover."

Louanne's face filled with anger. She struggled to control herself. "What do you know about the Bible or healing? I bet you've never even been inside a church."

She knew I was a lesbian. She detested me. Julia or no Julia, I was under no obligation to take shit from this fanatical, demagogic fruitcake. "Listen, I really don't give a flying —"

"Let us take her back to her room," Julia interrupted. "God is everywhere. You can continue the prayer without her."

"She has to claim the miracle," Louanne said.

"Lazarus was dead when he was healed. How did he claim his miracle?" Julia said.

Good biblical argument, kiddo, I thought gleefully. That's why I love you.

Louanne nodded but did not speak.

We walked back into the room.

"Sisters," Louanne said, "we're going to continue praying for Rachel now. Carla and Julia will take her back to her room."

Julia and I stood on either side of Rachel and slipped our arms around her.

"Come on, friend," I said. "We're going to take a little walk."

She looked into my eyes and nodded almost imperceptibly.

"Let's go," I said.

Julia and I walked her out of the room.

"Nice touch about Lazarus," I said to Julia.

"I've been arguing scripture with her for years," Julia said.

"What's your room number?" I asked Rachel.

"Two-seventeen," she replied faintly.

She let us nearly carry her to her room. The door was unlocked. We led her inside and guided her to the bed, where she sat and began rocking.

"Rachel, why don't you get dressed for bed?" I added to Julia, "Let's look for some pajamas."

As we dug through her dresser, I turned to see

Rachel had tied a scarf around her neck and was attempting to choke herself. I dashed across the room and pulled it away.

"Rachel," I said, "do you want to go to the hospital?"

"No, please," she muttered, "no more hospitals."

"You want to go to bed then?" I said.

"I can't stay here." Her plea was heart-rending.

I looked at Julia. "We've got to get her out of here."

"Carmen, we can't do that."

"Why are you calling me Carmen?" I said, giving her a glare that was anything but subtle.

"Where will we take her?"

"You see what's going on here. We've got to try and make a break for it. She'll go nuts under this pressure if we don't."

"What about Louanne?" Julia said.

That bitch out of the ninth circle of Dante's *Inferno* could kiss my ass on Main Street at high noon. "Louanne will have to take care of herself."

"Louanne's my family. I can't betray her."

"Do you want us to take you out of here?" I said to Rachel.

"Yes. Please," Rachel said.

"Well?" I said to Julia.

"Damn it," she said. "Let's go."

I turned to Rachel: "Get your stuff together. Bags, money, credit cards. You can stay at my place tonight, but then, we've got to think of something else."

Rachel sprang to life and gathered her belongings. A few minutes later, we were ready to go.

"Do you have a car?" I said.

"Daddy won't let me," Rachel said.

"Mine's right outside. You'll have to show us the safest way to get out of here."

As Julia and I picked up the bags, Rachel started to glaze over again. "Rachel," I said, "don't you fall apart on us. Pull yourself together."

"Wait a minute," Julia said. "Rachel, just write out a quick note that says you have to get away for a while, in case somebody gets worried."

"Good idea," I said.

"Okay," she muttered. "I want to go with you." She hurriedly scratched out a note.

The three of us headed down to the lobby.

A student guarding the front desk peered up from her copy of *Guideposts* magazine. "I'm sorry, ladies, but we're under curfew now. You can't leave the building again until six in the morning," she said.

"We're visitors," I said.

She stood up. "You two are ruining your chances of being admitted to this university."

Where was my flame thrower when I needed it? We kept walking.

"Rachel, I don't care if your father is a trustee. I still have to file a report on this," she said. "You go back now, and it's just between you and me."

Rachel froze.

"Rachel, come with us if you want," I said. "We're leaving." I snatched a pen from the guard's desk. "Give me your hand," I said to Rachel.

She extended her hand, and I wrote my home number on her palm.

"If you need me, give me a call," I said.

Julia and I headed outside. The campus was well-lit around Maranatha Hall, but soon we were submerged in darkness.

"Julia, look, I'm sorry. I don't want to cause trouble for you. You want me to talk to Louanne for you? I'll take the rap for everything," I said.

Julia didn't reply. We walked quickly toward the visitors lot. We were about halfway there when suddenly, I heard running behind us.

My heart pounding, I wheeled around. It was Rachel, struggling to catch up.

Rachel and Julia were silent as we sped away from the campus.

"Are you ever going to speak to me again?" I said to Julia.

"I don't want to get into a big discussion right now, Carmen."

She called me Carmen again. I hoped Rachel was too much of a zombie to notice. "Fine," I said. I wanted to pound the steering wheel, but I refrained, because of Rachel.

We didn't talk again until we neared the central part of the city. Julia said: "You want to drop me at the dorm?"

"Don't you want to stay with me?" I said. *Oh, Julia, please don't reject me. I don't do well with rejection.*

"I don't think so."

Don't panic. Don't beg. Let her have a night to herself. "Fine," I said. "If that's what you want."

As I pulled up in front of Mabel Smith Hall, I

touched Julia's arm. "Can I call you tomorrow?" I said. *Please let me call you.*

"I don't know," she said.

Oh shit, this hurt. Why did it have to be like this? I struggled to hold my emotions in check.

"Okay. See you later," I said, my voice breaking. "Good night." I watched her walk into the building.

Why did I have to be in love? Why hadn't I learned my lesson with Jane? I caught sight of Rachel in the rear-view mirror. It was a good thing she was sleeping, because I couldn't hold the tears back any more.

CHAPTER 7

When I awoke the next morning after a few hours of fitful sleep, Rachel was still out cold on the couch. She finally awoke while I was clearing away my breakfast dishes.

"Good morning," I said. "How are you doing?"

She looked small and fragile in the oversized striped red and white cotton pajamas I had given her. "I slept well for the first time in weeks."

"That's good to hear," I said. "If there's anything you want, just help yourself. I have English muffins, homemade strawberry jam, courtesy of my grandmother, and orange juice. Coffee's in a bag in the fridge. The grinder's on the counter." I thought it better to treat her like a responsible house guest rather than a head-case.

"Do you have any tea?"

"In the cabinet over the stove," I said.

Rachel heated the water while I washed dishes.

"Rachel, I have a confession to make."

"Yes?"

"I was never interested in attending LTU. I graduated a couple of years ago from FCU. I was there to meet you."

"Meet me? What for?" She backed away from me.

"I'm a journalist. My real name is Carmen Ramirez. I need to hide my identity because I don't want to lose my job. So please keep this between you and me. I am investigating your sister's murder. I don't think Diane Barrett did it, and I thought maybe you could tell me something about it."

More and more panic filled Rachel's face with each word. She began rocking nervously from foot to foot.

She was mixed-up, frightened, weak. It would be easy to break her down if I could make her feel obligated to me for rescuing her. "Calm down. Nobody's forcing you to talk to me. I didn't bring you here to grill you. I brought you here because I thought you were in danger."

She looked at me nervously.

"How do you get along with Mrs. Moffett?"

"How do you know about my grandmother?"

"I interviewed her. Maybe you should go stay with her until you decide what to do with your life.

Do you have anywhere else you can go until you get your head on straight? Any friends in town?"

"My grandma is just about it."

"Would you feel safe with her?"

"I think so," Rachel said.

"Then I'll take you out there today. I also think you need some mental health treatment."

"I've had all the treatment I can stand."

"That's up to you, of course, but I'll see what I can find out about mental health programs, in case you change your mind. Why don't you call your grandmother so she'll know you're on your way?"

She nodded.

Rachel was silent all the way out to Arrowhead. I didn't push her to talk. As we pulled into her grandmother's driveway, Mrs. Moffett peered out of the door. I could tell she was shocked to see me again.

"Your grandmother is fixing to pitch a big fit at me, so I'm going to leave in a hurry," I said to Rachel. "I've got a few things to tell you. Call me if you decide you're ready to talk about your sister. And let me know if you need anything from me. And take some time off from the Pentecostal Church. If you want to worship, try the Methodists or Episcopalians. I think a calmer church might do you some good right now."

Rachel nodded. "Thanks."

I handed her my phone number.

Mrs. Moffett charged out the door. She was

wearing the same housecoat and curler cap but had added a baseball bat to the ensemble.

"You get out of here," she screeched. "I've already called the sheriff."

"Mrs. Moffett," I said, "calm down."

"Get out," she screamed even more harshly.

"All right," I said. "We need to unload the car first."

She stood there wheezing and glaring as Rachel and I lifted the bags out of the car.

"Your granddaughter is in pretty rough shape," I said. "If you know what's good for her, you'll cut the histrionics and get her to a good doctor."

"Don't you be telling me what to do," Mrs. Moffett bellowed. "You're nothing but a gossip monger."

"That's a nice start," I said, shutting the hatch. "Remember what I told you, Rachel." I got in the car.

"Get out," Mrs. Moffett screamed again.

"No need to thank me," I said to her, pulling out of the driveway.

On the way out of Arrowhead, I was pulled over by a sheriff's deputy, a lumbering young cop with a red crew cut.

"Can I see your license, please, ma'am?"

I handed it to him.

"Your name's RAMMER-ez?" he said.

"That's pretty close."

"Why are you using an alias, ma'am?"

"I beg your pardon?"

"We got word of a gal name of Carla Sullivan harassing old Jeannie Moffett. Your tag number and description matches hers. Your name here is Carmen RAMMER-ez. That some kind of Mexican name?"

"It's a Spanish name," officer. "People of many nationalities have that name — among them, Mexicans."

"So how come you use two names? I can run you in, you know, and check you for priors."

I hesitated. "I just got married. I haven't had time to change my license yet. And Carla is short for Carmen," I said, hoping the big dope would buy it.

"Listen, Mrs. Sullivan, I'm going to let you go. You just stay clear of the Moffett place. That woman has had enough tragedy in one lifetime. You may be a hot tamale in Frontier City, but you're just a greaseball spic out here. You leave that woman and her granddaughter alone."

I nodded at the officer, memorized his name — Deputy Clyde Davis — and made a mental note to follow up with a civil rights complaint when I was through with my investigation.

All that Saturday and Sunday, I tried several times to reach Julia by phone, but she wasn't answering. And true to my word, I called the local Women's Center and tracked down some referrals for Rachel — if she was willing to take advantage of them.

Sunday night, I hit bottom — I started listening to Barbra Streisand. During my lonely teenage years, I had holed up in my room and I listened to Barbra for impossibly long stretches. I had believed that only her voice could express my deepest yearnings. I had been listening to Streisand for a couple of hours when the phone rang.

Hoping it was Julia, I turned down Babs and ran to the phone.

"Carmen?"

Oh shit. It was Jane. And I certainly wasn't in shape to talk to her. My heart was pounding. "Hi," I said, as casually as I could muster.

"How are you?" she said. "I've been thinking about you a lot lately."

"I'm just fine," I said. I wasn't about to tell her anything about Julia and me. "How are you?"

"Oh, busy. Really tired, too. Rita's been away a lot lately. She's handling some litigation in Kansas City."

Like I cared about what her bitch of a girlfriend was up to. So Jane was alone. Welcome to the club.

"So, Carmen, what's going on with you? You haven't written or called in so long."

I didn't respond.

"Carmen, I asked you a question."

I had dated a woman this pushy? "Jane, I haven't called or written because you hurt me."

"You chose to feel hurt, she said."

"I really don't need to hear this."

"We choose our feelings."

"Bullshit," I said. "Jane, there was a time when I loved you with every atom of my being. I idolized you. You were this brilliant, gorgeous Swede from the big city. I loved you in ways you could never understand."

132

"I never asked you to feel that way about me."

"Jesus Christ, woman, you were my first lover. What the hell did you expect?"

"You're getting hostile and abusive, Carmen."

"No, Jane. You're getting sadistic and manipulative. You never could control Rita, and she's obviously neglecting you."

"I don't need Rita to take care of me."

"Well, you called up for some reason. I think you were hoping to get a rise out of me, thinking I was still lovesick over you. You want to boost your ego at my expense."

"That's absurd."

"I don't think so," I said, my heart racing angrily. "Jane, I don't want to be in contact with you anymore. I'll never forget you. I couldn't. I loved you too much, and you were my first lover. But I don't want to talk to you anymore. Please respect that."

"You've met someone, haven't you?"

"Goodbye, Jane." I hung up on her.

For the first time, I had hung up on Jane.

I took a deep breath and called Charles. "It's Carmen."

"I'm glad you called. I was just getting ready to put on the Billie Holiday."

"Oh shit. I've been listening to Barbra. What's wrong?"

"Roger," he said. "He didn't want a relationship. At least that's what he told me today, when he finally called. He said I was getting too serious. So, we've broken up. And I'm headed to a Trappist monastery. Do you think they wear anything under those robes?"

I laughed. "Charles, you can't hit on monks."

"You want to make a bet?" he said. "So what's with you?"

"I just got off the phone with Jane."

"Oh my God, Carmen, no. What did that Dreadful Bitch have to say?"

"I guess Rita isn't paying enough attention to her, so she called me up to stir up the old hornet's nest."

"I hope you didn't fall for it."

"I asked her not to call me anymore. I think I'm finally over it."

"So why were you listening to Barbra?"

"Julia."

"Ah. So what's going on? I've been very curious."

"Well, we became lovers."

"You had sex?"

"Yes, Charles."

He squealed with prurient delight. I could just picture him with a naughty boyish grin on his handsome, swarthy face. "Did you remember how? Did something come to mind?"

"Shut up."

"Come, come, dear. You're far too modest about these things."

"That's enough," I said. "So now she won't talk to me."

"What happened?"

I filled him in on the conflict. "What should I do?"

"Shit. I don't know. Just give her some time. Sounds like she's really smitten with you. I think she'll be back."

"God, I hope so. I'm really in love."

"Carmen, why do you always have to fall like ten tons of bricks?"

"I wish I knew. Listen, I'm sorry about Roger. He must have been a pig to throw away a jewel like you."

"Thanks, dear."

I headed out to Crystal's to salve my wounds.

The bar was lonely that night. A few women were involved in raucous pool matches in the back room. The jukebox was silent; Crystal was playing taped music instead. I was nursing a Foster's lager and feeling very gloomy when a thought suddenly occurred to me: *Surely Diane, a heavy drinker and a lesbian, must have spent time in the city's only women's bar.* If I had been a comic book character, a light bulb would have appeared over my head.

Just then, Crystal moved over to me. She wore Levis and a red cowboy shirt with white piping. "What's up, kiddo?" she said as she wiped the bar in front of me. "You're not much of a drinker. You've been working on that beer for forty-five minutes."

"Sorry," I said. "Why don't you give me a seltzer with a twist of lime?"

"Sure," Crystal said.

I got out my wallet, but she waved away my money. "It's on the house," she said.

Did Crystal know anything about Diane? Could I work up the courage to question such a fierce-looking woman? "Thanks," I said as she handed me the drink. "This is kind of a slow night for you, isn't it?" I said, my voice sounding weak and frightened.

"Yeah, it ebbs and flows," she said, smiling. "But I have a steady enough clientele. Friday and Saturday are always the big nights. This old place has kept me in pork chops and beer for fifteen years." She let out a hearty laugh. "It's you teetotalers who are killing me."

"I could order ten shots of Jack Daniels and throw up on the floor if you like," I said, hoping she would laugh.

"Haw," Crystal chuckled. "I've seen that more than enough times, thank you, ma'am. Good God, the things I've found in that bathroom. We had one old gal slit her wrists. One of the patrons found her all sprawled out and bleeding like a stuck pig. When the paramedics got here, they didn't want to come in unless they had police backup. I told them it was attempted suicide, but they wouldn't have any part of it. I had to carry the gal out to the ambulance myself. Ruined a good shirt and pants too. Covered with blood."

"Listen, Crystal," I said. "You look like a straight shooter. I'm trying to dig up some information on a murder —"

She gave me a mocking, skeptical look. Her blue eyes turned hard. "You're awful young to be a homicide cop."

"I'm not with the police."

"I didn't think so," she said with a derisive laugh. "Private eye?"

"No. I work for the *Frontier City Times*."

"There's no lower form of life than a busybody," she said, turning her back and moving down the bar.

I started to panic, but I got off my stool and

followed her anyway. My words came out in a rush: "Listen, Crystal, I'm a copy editor. I'm trying to gather enough evidence to prove that my paper ran false information about someone. I'm trying to clear somebody's name — somebody I think was falsely accused."

"Who?"

"Diane Barrett. I think she was set up. Did you know her?"

"That's a possibility," Crystal said, glowering at me. "You got a press pass?" I showed her my ID badge from the *Times*. She studied it carefully. "Looks legit. You've been in here before. You really queer or just pretending?"

"I'm the real thing."

She looked at me hard. "I don't buy it."

"Look, Crystal," I said, "I give you my word I'm a lesbian. I also give you my word that I will not publish anything we talk about here. This will all be off the record if you like."

She folded her strong arms over her chest. "I've got nothing to hide. What do you want to know?" Crystal said.

"Did Diane come in here?" I showed Diane's photo to her.

"I don't need the picture. I got a real good memory. She was here plenty of times. She was a good customer. Too good, in fact. A lot of nights, I'd cut off the drinks. I can't tell you how many times I called taxis for her."

"Did she come alone?"

"For the most part. Sometimes another gal — a suicide blonde — would come looking for her. Real mother hen she was. Always drank Diet Pepsi. I'd rather drink piss. I'm a bourbon-and-branch woman, myself. Either that or an iced tea. But none of that diet shit for me. Anyway, I think her name was Opal or Jewel or something like that. Now see, I got to bragging on my memory, and I can't recall the name. The two of them made a lot of big scenes in here. Always trying to get Diane to leave the bar. More than once, I had to ask them to take it outside. What else you want to know?"

"Anything else stand out about her? Did anybody else look for her here?"

Crystal lit a filterless Camel cigarette and leaned on the bar. "Hmm. Well, one night, some man came out here looking for her. Sleazy-looking fellow with a big tattoo on his arm. Think it was a dragon or something. Made a big stink about how he was going to turn her in at school unless she saw things his way."

"What happened?"

"I threw him out. He never came back."

"You remember what he looked like?"

"White guy, tattoo, like I said, early forties. Starting to go bald. Big beer gut. He was mostly blubber. That's why I could muscle him out. Just pinned his arms back and he was a perfect gentleman." Planting her hands on her hips, Crystal smiled at the memory of her triumph.

I was impressed. I would never want Crystal to muscle me out of anyplace.

"Here's the real kicker for you, sweetheart," Crystal said. "I know Diane didn't kill that girl." She stubbed out her cigarette.

"How's that?"

"She was here the night the girl was killed. She was drunk as a skunk that night. I had one of the cocktail waitresses drive her home. But it was after closing time. Diane didn't get home until two-thirty, I would guess, and the papers said the time of death was early evening. Diane was here from happy hour, starting at four, until closing time. She was lapping up the booze like it was going out of style, the poor devil. And the waitress told me there was a man there that night at her house who helped Diane out of the car."

Hot damn, she was good. "Who was the man?"

Crystal paused to light another Camel. "The waitress didn't know. She didn't really pay much attention. I think she was afraid she was gonna get her ass kicked, so she made tracks out of there. I can't really blame her. No sense hanging around for a fight if you're not good with your fists. I've just always been gifted that way." She smiled again.

My heart was racing with excitement. "Did you say anything to the police?"

"Hell, I didn't have time. Diane snuffed herself 'fore I got a chance to say anything. Stupid, she was. Just plain dumb. After that, I called up the D.A.'s office, but they never did anything about the stuff I told them."

"What's the waitress's name?"

"Betty Martin," she said. "Damn good cocktail waitress, too. Could squeeze tips out of a corpse. She's long gone. Last I heard, she was out in Frisco. Sent me a postcard a while back — maybe a year. That's where all the kids want to go these days. They want to dress up like storm troopers and

French kiss on the sidewalks. I know a few bar owners out there. I could put out my feelers. She'll turn up. Everybody needs a watering hole."

"I would appreciate it," I said.

I slapped a twenty dollar bill and my business card on the bar.

"What's this for?"

"Just pretend I drank ten shots of Jack Daniels and puked on the floor. If you think of something else, call me."

"Shots go for three bucks apiece. You're a little short."

"You want more?"

Crystal laughed. "You kind of remind me of a little rabbit."

"How's that?"

"Cause you sure are easy to scare," she said, winking at me. "You don't have enough money to buy me. Put your wallet up. If you're trying to clear Diane, that's payment enough for me. She was a boozer, not a child molester. Believe you me, she wouldn't hurt a fly. And besides, the real killer is still out there."

"Thanks for all your help," I said.

"Watch yourself, kiddo. You're awful nervous to be in this line of work."

When I got home, the light on my answering machine was blinking. Hoping to hear Julia, I hit the replay button. I was stunned by a cruel, guttural, unfamiliar voice.

"If you want to stay healthy, keep your nose out of other people's business."

I was filled with panic. Immediately, I looked outside to see whether anyone was lurking, waiting to do me harm. I saw nothing. I dialed 911. The dispatcher assured me that an officer was on his way. Then I phoned Julia. I thanked God when she picked up on the second ring.

"I don't think I'm ready to talk to you," she said.

"Julia, please don't hang up. I received a threatening call tonight. I'm waiting for the cops right now."

"I'll be right over," Julia said.

"Don't walk. Somebody may be out there waiting for me."

"I'll get a ride. Don't worry."

A cop car arrived about two minutes later. But it seemed much longer.

With flashlights drawn, a pair of huge cops got out of their black-and-white and inspected the bushes surrounding my apartment. I noticed that old Mrs. Braun was peeking out of her window. One of the cops, an older man, approached me.

I led him into the house and I played the message for him as he took notes on a pad. Through the open front door, I saw Mr. Braun, clad in a plaid bathrobe, out talking with the cop's partner.

"Miss Ramirez, have you recently broken up with a boyfriend?"

"No," I said.

"Hooked up with a new boyfriend?"

"No."

He looked around the place. "Well, chances are,

this was just a one-time thing. Just a kook trying to throw a scare into you. I wouldn't worry about it."

"Officer, I'm a journalist, and I'm doing some investigative work. I think perhaps this threat is related."

"I doubt it."

"But he said for me to keep my nose out of other people's business."

"It's a common enough threat," he said.

Obviously, he didn't care about the threat.

I said, "You want to take the tape for evidence?"

"I don't think that will be necessary."

"You could do a voice print on it."

"We really don't have the resources to check out every crank call in a city this big. We'll keep an eye on you tonight. If anything else happens, let us know. We're only a phone call away."

I knew he was right, that they were doing all they could, but still, I was angry. Irrationally so. I wanted action. He returned to the cruiser. Mr. Braun, standing on his back porch, called out to me. "What's going on, Carmen?" he asked.

I told him.

"I'll keep an eye on you," he promised.

"Thanks," I said. I wondered what a frail man in his seventies could do to protect me.

A dark Volkswagen pulled up, and Julia hopped out. "Thanks a lot," she called out as the Bug sped off.

She came running over to me and Mr. Braun. "Carmen, are you okay? Where are the cops?"

"You just missed them," I said.

Julia and I walked into the apartment. I played the tape for her.

"God, that's creepy sounding." She looked tired, pale, and preoccupied. She had thrown on a tattered old T-shirt and some jeans before coming over. In her hurry, she hadn't even put on shoes.

I turned the tape over so that the message would be preserved.

"So why is this happening?" Julia said, with an edge of exasperation in her voice.

I told her what I had found out from Crystal.

"Don't you think you're getting in over your head? Why don't you just turn this information over to the police?"

"The police weren't interested two years ago. I don't think they will be now unless I find out more."

We stood there a while without talking.

Julia finally broke the silence. "Well, what do you want me to do?"

"Would you mind staying with me tonight?"

She sighed. "No. Not at all."

Later, we lay together in the same bed, but we did not touch. Julia seemed to drop off immediately.

Thoughts of the call tortured me. Deputy Clyde Davis knew my real name and — even with his limited intelligence — could easily have tracked down my number. He could have given Mrs. Moffett my number or made the call himself. Perhaps a third party had made the call at their urging. Hell, Moffett and the deputy might be related. Or maybe Rachel had turned on me. I had given her my number — maybe Mrs. Moffett had discovered it. Or maybe Rachel had turned against me thanks to some tirade from her grandmother. Rachel was unstable enough. The Rev. Metcalf was none too happy with me. But then again, he was a minister and ministers didn't usually do that sort of thing. I had given my real name and phone number to Crystal, but she didn't seem the type to make threatening calls. She would have just thrashed me on the spot. Or Louanne might have done it, angry that we had helped Rachel escape.

What about Julia? She might have persuaded one of her friends to help her get even with me for causing trouble for Louanne. But why would she come over when I called her? Guilty conscience? But she seemed to love me — even if she was angry with me. My own grandmother might have been behind it, to scare me into coming back home.

I played the list of suspects over and over until, at last, I fell into an uneasy sleep.

The next morning, Julia, who had helped herself to a pair of my sandals, was dressed and ready to leave when I awoke. I felt a guilty twinge for having even momentarily suspected her of making the call.

"Where are you going?" I said.

"Back to school. I have stuff to do."

"You want me to drive you over?"

"No. I'll walk."

"Were you just going to leave without saying anything?"

"Carmen, I'm sorry, but I'm having some problems right now."

"Can we talk about it?"

"No. I can't really. Not right now."

"Listen, I'm really sorry about Louanne. I didn't mean to come between the two of you."

"I can't discuss Louanne with you right now," she said. "I really have to go." She headed toward the door.

I felt tears welling up in my eyes. "This isn't fair to me. I wasn't the one who pushed this thing between us," I said. "You were the one who was in a hurry to get closer. And then, just when I let down my guard, you walk out. Well, I'll tell you what — I won't be a doormat for you or anybody else. You want to leave? Leave."

"I don't want to fight."

"Well, sometimes you have to," I shouted.

She walked over and sat on the bed. "Could you stop screaming?"

"All right," I said. "I'm sorry."

"Carmen, I'm not bailing out on you. I just need a little time to deal with some stuff." She reached out and touched my face gently. "I'll be back. I promise." She kissed me on the cheek.

CHAPTER 8

I returned to work Tuesday afternoon. I hadn't
heard from Julia since she'd left on Monday
morning. Six-day stretches awaited me this week and
the week after to make up for the nights I'd taken
off. I tried my hardest to keep my mind on commas
and colons instead of Julia as I pored through the
monotonous copy Sargent sent me.

At the end of the shift, I asked him about the
Barrett series.

"It's set to run next week. It'll start in next Sunday's paper."

"A week from this Sunday?"

"Yeah," Sargent replied.

"Thanks, Ralph," I said and left the newsroom.

When I got home, my answering machine was blinking. Nervous as hell, worried that new threats awaited me, I sat on the couch with the cats next to me for support and played back the messages.

"Carmen, this is Crystal Reeves of Crystal's Tavern. I tracked down Betty Martin. She's still in Frisco. I think she'll talk. Call me and I'll give you the details. Bye now."

The recorder beeped and a second message began.

"Hi, this call is for Carla Sullivan. I'm Ruby Weller. You can reach me at home. . . ." She left the number.

I called the bar and got the information on Betty Martin from Crystal, who asked me to keep her posted on all new developments. I tried Betty's number, but there was no answer and no machine. I decided to wait until the next morning to call Weller. It was too late at night to call a schoolteacher.

Just as I was ready to turn in, I heard rapping at the door. My heart pounded in fear. Perhaps it was my threatening caller, come to pay a visit. The cats dived under the bed. I threw on my bathrobe, picked up my trusty softball bat, and headed to the door.

"Who's there?" I bellowed in my most menacing voice.

"Carmen, it's me, Julia."

I opened the door. She stood there with a duffel bag. "Good God, you scared the life out of me. What are you doing here?" My body was racing with adrenalin — from the joy of seeing her and from fear.

"Look, Carmen, I'm sorry. Can I come in?" She was breathing hard.

We sat on the couch. She wore tattered gray sweat pants, a blue T-shirt, and decrepit tennis shoes. "How did you get here?"

"I walked. Actually, I ran."

"Jesus Christ, Julia," I said furiously, "There's a rape about every three seconds in this town, I've just been threatened, and you're walking the streets at night alone."

"I had to see you."

"Don't do that again. I'll pick you up. Or take a cab, for God's sake," I said.

"Listen, I have to tell you something."

The tone of her voice distracted me from my anger. She seemed upset and agitated. Her green eyes were bloodshot, and her face was puffy. "Is something wrong?" I put my arm around her.

She sighed and ran her hand through her short blonde hair. "Where should I start? At the beginning, I guess. Oh, God, this really sucks. Things have blown up with my family," she said gravely.

"How so?"

"When we were at LTU, Louanne figured out immediately that we were a couple. She was looking at me strangely; I knew something was up. We've always been that way with each other. Saturday, she called and asked me what was going on between the two of us. I couldn't lie to her — she's very perceptive. So I told her I was in a relationship with you."

I was stunned, but I didn't want to add to Julia's agitation. I kept my reaction calm. "I see."

"Well, she freaked out, and hit me with all this Bible stuff. Told me that homosexuals would have no share in the kingdom of God. All that good stuff."

"I've heard the same stuff. Believe me," I said. I wanted to kick the shit out of that Bible-thumping maniac.

"That's not the worst of it. She's told my parents."

"Holy shit," I said. She and all the other people who consign their fellow creatures to hell in the name of a loving God ought to be locked up.

"They called tonight. They're very upset. They're driving up tomorrow. They want me to come home with them." Julia rubbed her forehead nervously.

"Oh no," I said. My heart froze. *Please don't go. Please, God, don't let her leave me.*

"They want me to leave FCU immediately and go to the University of Arkansas next semester. Otherwise, they're going to cut my money off."

"Oh my God, Julia. I'm so sorry I got you into all this," I told her.

Nice going, Carmen, I raged at myself. You turned a promising student and model daughter into a penniless outcast and reprobate overnight. No, on second thought, don't feel guilty. That's just what Louanne and her type want.

"Please don't apologize," Julia said. "I love you. I'm not going back." She made a fist to emphasize her words.

She's staying. She loves me again. Thank you, God. "What can I do to help?"

"This semester is paid for. I have a partial scholarship. I guess I'll have to see whether I can go to school part time and finish out my degree here. I have the internship at the *Times*. Maybe they'll keep me on as a clerk after the semester is out."

"Maybe so."

"There's no way I'm leaving FCU in my junior year. I was planning to graduate a semester early anyway. I think I can manage it. I don't know what I'm going to do. I'm going to talk to my adviser and see what options are open to me."

"That sounds like a good plan."

"You know, having your entire family turn on you is terrible, Carmen. I'm their only child. We've always been so close."

I hugged her tightly. "I know. It's happened to me. And it hurts. I wish it could have gone smoother. Give them time. I think they'll be a little better about it. Grandma's not great about it, but she's finally stopped throwing hatchets at me."

Julia managed a laugh. "I have a favor to ask."

"Sure. Anything."

"I need to hide out while my parents are in town. I left a message for them at the dorm that I didn't want to see them. I told them I was staying off campus. Can I stay here?"

"Sure, if you think that's the best thing. It might just make them angrier," I said.

"I can't face them right now. Don't you want me here?"

"Of course I do, my love." I kissed her forehead and stroked her gently. "But maybe you ought to call them or meet them for lunch or something. They're driving all the way from Arkansas."

"I don't know. I'll call the dorm tomorrow morning and see how they are," she said. Suddenly, she stood up and clapped her hands. She paced around the room as her words tumbled out. "Listen, I've got it. Every summer since I was fifteen, I've worked in my parent's store. My mother's been investing the money for me all this time. I'll make them hand it over. I worked for it. I ran the cash register, stocked the shelves, helped unload trucks. I even wore one of those nail aprons. I did it all. They owe it to me. I can pay off my school."

"Good."

There was a moment of silence. Julia sat back down beside me and touched my face gently. "I'm sorry I was so weird to you. I know I hurt your feelings. I do love you and I want you to be my sweetie. I should have let you know what was going on. I just didn't know what to do. I mean, they are my family and all. I'm all they have. This is a tough choice to make."

"It's okay. We'll talk about it later. Let's get to sleep now — we have a lot to do tomorrow."

She kissed my neck. Oh, how I loved this woman. And she was back.

* * * * *

Early the next morning, Julia called the dorm and left my number with the front desk for her parents. She headed for the shower and I called Ruby Weller, who reluctantly agreed to meet me Sunday afternoon. As soon as I hung up, the phone rang.

"Julia Nichols," a man with a back-woods Arkansas accent said.

This must be Daddy. "She can't come to the phone right now. May I take a message?"

"What have you done with her?"

"I beg your pardon?"

"You're the creature who's dragged her into a life of sin, aren't you?" In the background, I heard a woman say, "Bob, please."

"Sir, I'm not going to talk to you anymore. I'll have Julia call you as soon as possible. Where are you?"

"We're at the school, where she's supposed to be." He hung up.

This was not going to be pretty.

Julia met her parents for breakfast at the Fifteenth Street Diner. She returned to the apartment after less than an hour. Her face was splotchy red.

"What happened?" I said.

"I'm not going back with them and they're cutting off my money. That's it. My mother has agreed to hand over the investment income to me, though. She seems a little more reasonable than my father. Other than that, they refuse to endorse a life

152

of sin. And you know what else? Dad kept complaining that he'd had to leave the store for a day and he was going to be behind in his work."

The bastards. Parents were always so supportive at times like these. I guess they'd prefer her to be screwing with some pimply little frat boy in a BMW. "I'm sorry," I said.

"You and me both," Julia said.

Julia returned to campus that afternoon to sort out her financial affairs and return to her studies. We planned to see each other Monday evening and to stay in touch by phone.

I finally reached Betty Martin on Friday afternoon, after trying to reach her at every hour of the day.

"Your name was given to me by Crystal Reeves of Crystal's tavern in Frontier City."

"How is old Crystal?" she said with enthusiasm.

"Fine. Fine."

"She's really the sweetest woman you'd ever want to work for. Takes real good care of all of her waitresses."

"Betty, I'm investigating the murder of Rebecca Metcalf. Crystal tells me that you drove the prime suspect, Diane Barrett, to her house the night of a murder."

"You a cop?"

"No, a journalist. Crystal helped me by giving me your name. I think Diane was framed."

"I'll say she was."

"Why?"

"Because she was dead drunk that night. She had been drinking all day, since the start of happy hour, and didn't leave till after closing time. That's two back in Frontier City. I took her home because it was on my way and she was a regular. A real good tipper. Besides, Crystal asked me to."

"So what happened that night?"

"Well, she was dead drunk, like I said. I pulled up into the driveway. This guy was there, a friend of hers, I guess. He helped her out of the car. That's about all I hung around for."

"What did he look like?"

"It was dark, and I didn't want to hang around. I'm a cocktail waitress, not a social worker."

"So you don't remember anything about him? Was he black, white, short, tall? Moles, scars, tattoos? Anything at all."

"He was white and had dark hair, kind of in a Three Stooges haircut."

"Which Stooge?"

"The one with the bangs."

"Do you remember anything else?"

She hesitated. "No. Nothing really stands out in my mind. He called her by name and helped her out of the car. He wasn't violent. She didn't seem afraid of him, so I let him take her. I'm sorry. I don't really have Crystal's memory."

"You've helped quite a bit. Listen, if you think of anything else, let me know."

Betty said, "I should warn you — Crystal tried to get something done about this a couple of years ago, but nobody wanted to hear about it."

"I hope this time it'll be different."

* * * * *

Sunday afternoon, Ruby Weller greeted me at her front door. "Hi," she said nervously. "Come on in."

The house was plain and simple. Its white walls were covered with varnished, unstained shelves, full of years of learning. Ruby was tall and athletic, her dyed blonde hair short and permed. Her eyes were dark brown, her face thin, pale, and full of worry. She wore an old gray sweat suit. A can of Diet Pepsi sat on the end table next to the couch.

"What's this all about?"

Ruby and Diet Pepsi. She must be Opal or Jewel, the suicide blonde Crystal was talking about.

As we sat on the couch, I quickly collected my thoughts. She wasn't going to open up unless I was direct with her. "Ms. Weller, I'm going to have to trust you with some information. I think I can."

"Go ahead," she said. "And please call me Ruby."

"In the first place, I don't work for the *Herald*, but I am a journalist. And my name isn't Carla Sullivan. I'm Carmen Ramirez. I'm a copy editor for the *Frontier City Times*. I'm putting my job on the line by telling you this," I said, showing her my ID badge from the *Times* and my driver's license. "My paper is preparing a series on the Barrett case. Personally, I think Diane was framed because she was a lesbian and a convenient target, and I think you can help me prove that."

"I don't know what this is all about, but I think you'd better leave." She stood up.

"I'm taking a shot in the dark here. Have you ever gone to Crystal's on the East Side with Diane?"

155

"I've never heard of the place," she said. Her deep blushing told me otherwise.

"I've interviewed the bar owner, Crystal. The woman has a memory like an elephant. She says a blonde woman with a name like yours came to the bar and tried to get Diane to lay off the booze and go home. She even remembered that this patron always drank Diet Pepsi."

She looked guiltily at the can of Pepsi. "A lot of people have blonde hair and drink Diet Pepsi. I don't know what you're talking about."

"Ruby, it's easy enough for me to pick up a photograph from the school and run it past Crystal. I'm sure she'll remember your face."

"What the hell are you trying to do? That's a gay bar, and this is Oklahoma. Are you trying to run me out of my job?" She was trembling.

"I'm not going to say anything to endanger you or your job. I don't care that you went to a gay bar. You might as well know, I'm a lesbian. That's why I knew to check with Crystal. Would a straight girl think to check there? And even if she did, do you think Crystal would give her anything but the boot? I'll leave your name out of this — I promise. I won't let you be tied in with this in any way," I said. "Please help me."

Her face turned deeper red and she sighed. Finally, she said: "Why should I trust you?"

"Because I've given you enough information on me to get me fired in about ten seconds. You could call up my supervisor, Ralph Sargent, and he could make sure I never work in this town again. You want his number?"

She didn't reply. She looked lost in thought.

"Look, I can't force you to talk to me. But doesn't it bother you that Rebecca's killer is still free and Diane is dead? Crystal is willing to testify that on the night of the murder, Diane didn't leave the bar until after the time the coroner said Rebecca was killed. And I have a cocktail waitress who's willing to testify Diane was too drunk to drive. She drove Diane home that night, after closing time," I said. "Will you please help me?"

"All right," she said, sinking back into the couch. She looked defeated.

"What kind of relationship did you and Diane have?"

She began to cry. "We were friends," she said. "This is very hard for me."

"Take your time."

"She drank so much. She was sick and helpless in a lot of ways, but I loved her. I wanted to fix things for her. I suppose that says a lot about me. Sometimes, she'd come over to my place. She was so sad so much of the time. And I loved her so much. I'd always take her in and try to comfort her. Sometimes, it was physical. But she never stayed."

Should I push on? Ruby's body was heaving with sorrow. She had been holding a lot in for the past two years. It might do her good to tell her story.

She walked to the bathroom, and I could hear her running water and blowing her nose. She returned with a box of Kleenex.

"Sorry about that," she said, her voice still shaky. "This still hurts. A lot."

"I know it must be rough for you."

She gave me a weak smile.

"Did Diane's drinking ever affect her work?"

"She was always cold sober around the children. They were her life."

I waited awhile, out of respect. "Any men in her life?"

"Funny you should ask," Ruby said, pulling a Kleenex out of the box and quickly crumpling it. "The head janitor, Buddy Jefferson, used to slobber all over her. But he slobbered all over anybody with a pulse."

"That's interesting. He told a reporter from the *Times* that she didn't have any use for men."

"That slime bag," Ruby said. "He'd rat on his own mother if he thought it would make him look good."

"What kind of relationship did they have?"

"Diane had a talent for finding people who would mistreat her," she said, the tears flowing again. "He helped her start her car once after school one day. Then he wouldn't leave her alone. They went out drinking a couple of times, and then she couldn't get rid of him. Finally, she told him she was gay — even that didn't stop him. I guess it must have turned him on. She just stopped talking to him altogether. She started getting obscene phone calls. They didn't let up until she died."

"How do you know it was him?"

"Diane's number was unlisted, and she changed it a lot. But the school always had it, and Buddy has a key to every lock in the building."

"Did she ever report it?"

"Yeah. She talked to the principal about it. Hawkins confronted him, he claimed complete innocence. So there was nothing she could do. Or so she said."

"Does Buddy have a big belly and a dragon tattoo on his arm?"

"Yeah. Why do you ask?"

"Crystal says a man fitting that description followed Diane to the bar one night. Crystal threw him out."

"He used to follow her around everywhere. He enjoyed stalking her. Making her nervous. Here's something else for you," she said, her voice rising. "Buddy's assistant, Bill Jones, told me he had uncovered a whole bunch of hard-core pornography in the supply room. Bill went straight to Hawkins with the stuff. He said that Buddy gave him the creeps and he was sure the porn belonged to him. He told her he didn't think somebody like that should be working around children."

"So what happened?"

"Hawkins told him that she had no proof the pornography belonged to Buddy. She said Bill himself might have planted the pornography — just to make Buddy look bad."

"You think he might have?"

"It's possible. The two of them didn't get along all that well. Bill is black. Buddy is a racist redneck."

"Did you see the stuff?"

"Bill told me that Hawkins ordered him to throw it in the incinerator. It must have been bad to shock Bill. He's an ex-Marine, combat veteran. He served in Vietnam. He's been through some rough stuff. What could shock him?"

"Kiddie porn?" I suggested.

"Bill wouldn't tell me anything about it. He just said, 'It's sick. You don't want to know.' "

I tried to picture this porno-hoarding obscene caller. What might he have been capable of? "Do you think Buddy might have molested Rebecca?"

Ruby scratched her head. "I just don't know."

"Have you ever seen him speaking to any of the little girls?"

"I haven't. But Bill keeps a closer eye on him than I do. Bill's a good guy. We go way back. He'll tell you all he can. Let him know you're a friend of mine."

"Could you get me phone numbers for the two men?"

Ruby fetched a faculty-staff directory from near the phone. "Keep that. I can get another copy at school. You'd better watch yourself around Buddy."

"I'll be careful."

Actually, I had no idea of how to approach either of them, but I wanted to retain my aura of professionalism. I was relieved that Ruby seemed so concerned about my welfare and so willing to help.

"What happened to Diane's belongings?"

She grimaced. "Her scumbag brother and his wife took the stuff that was valuable. Her voice had turned bitter again. There was no will. They hadn't been in touch with her for years because she was a queer. They were proper church folk, you see. They didn't even want her ashes — too tainted by the queer influence, I guess. Just her money and jewelry. So I have all her personal stuff."

"May I see it?"

Ruby eyed me warily. Perhaps I had pushed too

far. Perhaps she began to realize how much she had told me.

"Listen, if you're not comfortable with it —"

"Come on with me. It's in the spare room."

I followed her through a hallway to a small, neat bedroom. "Her books are on the shelf. I arranged them over there," she said.

I walked to a large pine bookcase filled with teaching texts, as well as books of history, child psychology, and popular fiction. On a middle shelf a framed photograph of Diane, happy and smiling, was next to a green porcelain urn with a small brass plaque inscribed *Diane Marie Barrett, 1941-1983, Teacher and Beloved Friend.* To the side was a small vase holding a tiny pink rose. I studied the photograph.

"I took that picture back at a faculty-student picnic in 'seventy-nine. Diane's students loved her. And so did I." She was weeping again. "She didn't hurt that little girl."

I nodded and returned the photo to the shelf. I was moved by the depth of her love for Diane and embarrassed to be treading on her privacy.

Ruby opened the closet and dragged out a trunk. "This is mostly her personal papers. Old grade books, photo albums, letters. I have it arranged in folders. I couldn't bear to throw it away."

"I'll be very careful with it," I said.

Ruby sat on the bed and watched as I sat on the floor and carefully pulled out folders and laid them on the floor. I opened a grade book. At once, I could tell that Diane was a careful teacher. Color-coding the class roll, she had underlined in red the name the student preferred to be called. I thumbed

161

through a couple of books before I found Rebecca Metcalf's records, which showed spotty attendance and grades that ranged from A to F.

"Did she ever talk to you about Rebecca's schoolwork?"

"We all had problems with that girl," Ruby said. "Rebecca was in my class the year before. She was a brilliant, emotional kid — very erratic. Every year, the teachers would recommend that Rebecca be evaluated by one of the district psychologists. Hawkins contacted the father. He always said Christian discipline could cure her problems."

"I guess this won't come as a shock to you, but Hawkins told me Rebecca was a normal kid with no major discipline problems."

I continued looking through the papers. Diane had saved several drawings her students had made. Houses, sunny skies, horses, dogs — bright crayon drawings on newsprint.

In the bottom of the pile, I found Diane's yearbooks from FCU. "Did you know her back then?" I asked.

"No," Ruby said. "I didn't meet her till I started working at Washington. I came here a year after she did."

Thumbing through Diane's freshman yearbook, I found her photo in the posh Chi Delta sorority.

"Diane was in a sorority?"

"Yeah, till they threw her out. She was caught necking with another girl in her room. I think they were more upset because the girl she was with wasn't even Greek."

On the next page, I found a shot that nearly knocked me over. Diane posed with a strangely familiar beau in a photograph of the annual Pan-Hellenic, Interfraternal Ball. I checked the caption. "I don't believe this. It's Ron Blazer."

It was indeed Ron Blazer, member of Sigma Phi fraternity. He was easily recognizable. He was wearing the same unattractive bowl-cut hairdo he still wore today.

"Another asshole who clung like a leech to her," Ruby said. They went out during her first couple of years of college. Ron just wouldn't let go, even when the scandal hit and Diane got thrown out of the sorority. He pursued her throughout college. I think she saw him on and off for years. She never got free of him."

"Holy shit!" I exclaimed. "Blazer works for the *Times*. He was the original reporter on the murder and he's an assignment editor now. He destroyed Diane in his articles. This is some kind of vendetta for him. The cold-hearted son of a bitch!"

"I never put him together with the newspaper. I couldn't bear to read the stories or watch TV."

I shook my head. "I wonder whether he's the guy Betty Martin was talking about?"

"Who's Betty Martin?"

"A cocktail waitress who used to work at Crystal's. She drove Diane home the night of the murder. There was a man at Diane's house that night who helped her out of the car. Betty didn't get a good look at him, because she was scared. But she did remember his Three Stooges haircut. It's gotta be Blazer. Maybe the police could jog her memory with a photo."

Just then, I found a stack of letters held together with a rubber band. All were from Blazer. I opened one from 1982. It was written in a wild, loose scrawl.

My Dearest Di:
I can't tell you how many times I pray that you can see how much I love you. The thought of you choosing a life of perversion over a respectable life with the man who loves you sickens me to the core.

Why can't you find it in your heart to discover the beautiful life we could have together? Only I can take care of you.

If you turn your back on the laws of Nature and the laws of man, you open yourself up to a life of danger. Your sick friends cannot protect you.

I am filled with rage when I think of all the nights I have spent without you. You must turn back before it is too late.

This guy was a bona fide sicko.

"Listen, Ruby," I said, "you need to guard these letters carefully. I don't know what Ron is capable of. I think you ought to put this stuff in a safe deposit box, just to be sure."

"Why?"

"Because these letters destroy his journalistic credibility. If this stuff ever became public, he'd lose his job. Does he know you have them?"

"I wouldn't know. I've never had any direct contact with him."

I opened more of Blazer's letters. They were all pretty much the same, alternating between whining pleas and threats. And always filled with sick rage.

"God almighty," I said as a chill ran through me. "This man is frightening."

"Should I be worried?" Ruby said.

"If he hasn't bothered you by now, he probably won't — unless he knows you have these letters."

Ruby nodded.

"And from the tone of these letters, Blazer seems sick enough to have made the phone calls."

That afternoon at the newsroom, I had an hour to spare before my shift. It was time to go to Sargent with what I had learned. I was feeling anything but triumphant. The tragedy of this case overwhelmed any joy over proving Sargent wrong. Besides, I needed his help. I had to persuade him that Blazer was unethical and that the series had to be stopped.

I called Sargent's home. Mrs. Sargent informed me that he was gone on a fishing trip in Missouri and wouldn't be back until Tuesday. Knowing Sargent, I was sure fishing was just an excuse for sitting out in a bass boat all day and drinking beer. I asked her to have him call me as soon as he returned. Then I phoned Bill Jones. I introduced myself as a friend of Ruby Weller's.

He was immediately friendly. "What can I do for you?"

I heard a woman in the background call out: "Who is it, Billy?"

"A friend of Ruby's."

"So," I proceeded, "I'm investigating the death of Rebecca Metcalf."

"You a cop?"

"No. I work for the *Frontier City Times*."

His voice turned formal. "We're fixing to leave for church, ma'am."

"I just want a couple of minutes, Mr. Jones. Ruby told me that you found some pornography that belonged to Buddy Jefferson at the school."

"She told you that?"

"Yes, sir. Was it kiddie porn?"

"Some of it was. The man has a taste for everything. S&M mainly. The real rough stuff."

"I see. Do you think he might have molested any of the kids at the school, including Rebecca?"

"I don't know about that. I keep an eye on the fellow as much as I can. I don't trust him at all. I don't know what he does at home, but I don't think he could have gotten away with it at the school."

"You're sure?"

"Like I said, I never saw him get away with nothing with the kids," he said. "Look, Miss Ramirez, my wife and I are expected at the church. We're bringing a covered dish to the picnic, and we can't be late. And you stay away from that man. He's bad news, let me tell you."

"I understand. Thanks for your help."

I phoned Buddy. Living up to his sleazy billing, he refused to be interviewed over the phone and asked to meet me at a strip club. Finally, I agreed to meet him Monday at 3:30 p.m. at the bar of the Frontier Plaza Hotel downtown. It was well-lit and filled with respectable business types. I figured nothing could happen to me there.

166

Just before my shift started, I walked over to Terry Harris, the only female police reporter on the paper's staff. We had never been friends, but I knew her from journalism school. A brunette with shoulder-length permed hair, she had a pleasant enough face and always wore a lot of makeup; outside the office, she chain-smoked Marlboros. She was wolfing down a Texas ham and cheese sub from the Speedy Petey and listening to the police scanner. "Hi, Carmen," she said between bites.

"Hey, Terry, I was wondering whether you could do me a favor. Could you get one of your police contacts to check somebody out for priors? William Harold 'Buddy' Jefferson." I had gotten his full name from the directory Ruby had given me.

"Prospective boyfriend?" she said as she wrote the name on a note pad.

"Hardly," I said.

"Well, I have a couple of pals who can do it, but they aren't in today. You in a big hurry for it?" She finished the last of her sandwich in a huge bite.

"I need it by tomorrow, before three."

"I can call either of these guys up tomorrow when their shifts start around ten. If I go through normal channels, it could take up to a week. So what's up, Miss Copy Desk?"

"I can't tell you anything about it right now."

"What's in it for me?"

"You're helping a fellow journalist?"

"I don't think so."

"What do you want?"

"A Frito pie from Nick's."

Nick's was one of the greasiest eateries in town. It specialized in chili dogs. "You're on."

"I'll get back to you by three."

Monday afternoon, I got ready for my meeting with Buddy. I dressed as conservatively as possible — a long-sleeved shirt buttoned all the way to the top and some khaki slacks. After a prolonged argument, Julia had agreed to act as my watchdog during the meeting.

At 2:45, the phone finally rang.

"Carmen, Terry. Zippo. The computers have been down for two hours at the police department. I won't hear anything back until four. You still want the info?"

"Sure. Thanks a lot, Terry."

"Sorry, Carmen."

I deliberated my next move. What if this guy was a real sicko? After all, he was a porn aficionado. I already strongly suspected him of making obscene calls. Should I ask him whether he had murdered Rebecca Metcalf? Did I expect him to say yes?

On the other hand, he didn't know my real name and I'd be in a public place, with Julia to back me up with a call to 911 in case things got rough.

I had to go ahead.

At 3:00 p.m., I stood waiting for Julia outside Westman Hall. She came bounding out at 3:05.

"What did you find out about the creep?"

"Nothing. The police computers were down."

"Carmen," Julia said angrily.

"Listen, let's go. I'm going to be late."

"I don't think you should go."

"Please. I can handle it."

"The other day, weren't you giving me a lecture about walking the streets at night? And now you're going to meet up with some pervert?"

She had a point. "Julia, I know what I'm doing." Actually, I didn't, but it sounded good.

We arrived downtown. I parked at a garage several blocks away from the Plaza, because I didn't want Mr. Pervert following me to my car and tracking me down through my license plate.

Julia and I arranged a signal if anything went wrong at the table. I would put my sunglasses in my shirt pocket to let her know she should call for help. Julia went into the lounge first. I waited in the lobby for Buddy.

Seemingly out of nowhere, I heard a voice. "Hey, good-looking."

I turned around, and there was a greasy, balding man standing behind me.

"Buddy?"

He leered at me. "You got me, baby. All you can handle."

I looked at him in horror. He was wearing a stained sports shirt over his big beer gut and filthy plaid pants. He had a tattoo of a dragon on his arm. Crystal's memory was uncanny.

"Nervous?"

"No," I lied. "Why do you ask?"

"Well, I like fear. It's a turn-on. Besides, I noticed you brought your little friend with you. Were you looking for a little three-way action?"

The way he looked at me made me feel dirty. "This interview is canceled," I said emphatically.

"Oh, you're breaking my heart, baby. You met me here, and we're going to have our little date as planned."

"Get lost," I said.

He put his hand on my arm. His grip tightened and he said: "You're coming with me."

I firmly planted my feet and looked around me. A man in a red jacket was working at the front desk. Buddy began dragging me away. "Hey you, clerk," I shouted.

The Red Jacket man looked up from his work and walked over. "What seems to be the problem here?"

"Call the police," I said. "This man is attempting to drag me away against my will."

"Nonsense," Buddy said, laughing. "This is just a little lovers' quarrel."

Red Jacket looked at us contemptuously. "We don't want any problems here. Why don't you people take your dispute elsewhere?"

"Please call the police," I shouted.

Buddy finally released his grip. He looked at me mockingly: "You can't prove a thing, you bitch."

Buddy sauntered out of the hotel.

Suddenly, I felt something touch my shoulder. I screamed.

"Carmen, relax, it's me," Julia said. "What happened?"

"Things got out of hand with Buddy." I was shaking badly.

"Let's go home." She led me out of the hotel, but I was sure that Buddy was somewhere out there waiting. I stood in front of the hotel, as if rooted to the sidewalk.

"Come on, Carmen. Let's go."

"I cant."

"Listen, as soon as you get home, you're going to feel better."

I followed her to the garage. She assured me no one had followed us. I drove home, taking a circuitous route. As we arrived home, the phone was ringing. Julia took the call, spoke briefly, and hung up.

"That was Terry, from the paper. Buddy Jefferson has been arrested seven times, with two convictions — statutory rape and aggravated sexual assault. He did six months in Frontier County Jail on the first, three years in McAlester on the second. His record's been clean for the past twenty years, though."

"What a comfort that is," I said.

I got little sleep that night. My heart kept racing with fear over my encounter with Buddy. The next morning, still stinging with fear and shame, I told myself I had to get moving. Julia returned to campus after many reassurances from me that I was feeling better. After all, Buddy didn't know who I was or where I lived, so I was safe, I told myself.

There was still work to be done, and I wasn't going to let him keep me from it.

The first order of business was to call Dr. Hawkins. After an initial runaround from her secretary, I got through to the principal.

"I have something to tell you about one of your employees, Buddy Jefferson. I don't think he should be working around children."

"Oh, yes, Miss Sullivan," she said in a weary tone, "and on what are you basing this piece of slander?"

"The fact that he has two convictions on sexual offenses."

Hawkins stammered unintelligibly for a moment. Finally, she blurted: "Where did you find this out?"

"The Police Department. It's a matter of public record."

Hawkins stammered, "What do you intend to do with this information?"

"I'm sure the school board and the PTA would be interested. I'm trying to see that children are protected. Why did you continue to let him work at the school after Bill Jones, his fellow janitor, found hardcore pornography on the premises?"

"I have no comment," Hawkins said.

"He's still a very dangerous man. He exhibited aggressive behavior toward me. Why do you let him work there?"

She didn't answer.

"Did he kill Rebecca Metcalf?"

Dr. Hawkins hung up.

* * * * *

I phoned Ralph Sargent that afternoon, before work. This time, he was at home.

"Ralph, I have some very disturbing news, and I didn't want to wait until I got to work to tell you."

"Don't keep me in suspense."

I took a deep breath. "After you took me off the Barrett series, I kept digging on my own because I knew something was fishy."

"Goddammit to hell —"

"Hold on, Ralph. I have solid proof that Diane didn't commit the murder. I think Ron Blazer set her up because he has an ax to grind with her."

"What the hell are you saying? I've known Ron Blazer for years. He's a solid professional."

Could the old-boy network ever be wrong? How could it, when it ran on pure testosterone? "Ralph, would you just be quiet and listen to somebody else talk." My voice was fierce. I wasn't going to let him intimidate me into silence.

"Now you hold on just a goddamn minute. How dare you —"

"Ralph, if you don't want to listen to me, I'll go all the way to the publisher if I have to."

"Carmen, you can't just —"

"If the publisher won't listen, I'll go to the *Herald.*"

There was silence. Finally, he spoke in a strange, subdued voice. "Go ahead. Say what you have to say. But I warn you —"

"No warnings, Ralph. Just listen." My heart was pounding but at least I had his attention.

He was absolutely silent as I filled him in on the case in calm, measured tones.

"Now you've heard it," I concluded. "What do you think?"

"Jesus H. Christ," he said, returning to his bullying tone. "You've seen the letters, Carmen? You know they exist?"

"Yes, Ralph. I'd stake my job, my reputation, my life on it."

"You've already staked your job on it."

"That can't be helped," I said. "I'd rather be a file clerk than work for a dishonest newspaper. Hell, I'd rather scrub toilets at the bus station."

"You may well get your wish," he said. "Where the hell are the letters?"

I ignored his threat. "I can't reveal that."

"Why not, goddammit?"

"Because I don't know what Blazer is capable of. He could be very dangerous."

He was silent.

"Their picture was taken together at a college ball. They were definitely sweethearts. A source told me he'd been harassing Diane for years. And a witness says a man matching Ron's description was at Barrett's house the night of the murder. He's in this up to his neck."

After a long silence, Sargent said: "Don't do anything with this information till I get back in touch with you. I'll take it from here."

"All right, Ralph," I said. "Do I still have a job? Should I bother to show up?"

There was no hesitation. "Hell, yes, you'd better show up. We've got a goddamned paper to put out, Carmen." And with that, he hung up.

* * * * *

For the next couple of hours, I tried to rest, but I couldn't, because I was tortured by fears. Could Sargent be trusted? Would I lose my job for defying him? Would Ruby be safe? Had I gotten myself into more danger?

The ringing of the phone shook me from my thoughts.

"It's Rachel."

"How are you doing?"

"Fine, I guess. Actually not so fine." Her voice sounded strange and remote. "It's all closing in on me. I can't control it any more."

"What is?"

"Everything."

"Rachel, where's your grandmother?"

"She's not here."

"Where are you?"

"In a motel."

"What motel?"

"I'm not going to tell you."

"Why not?"

"I know too many dirty little secrets. And dirty secrets leave dirty little handprints all over your mind."

"Rachel, what's going on?"

"Carmen, you're the only one who can know. I'm not going to live much longer."

"Are you going to hurt yourself?"

She didn't reply.

"Tell me where you are. Now!"

She hung up.

For a moment, I panicked. Then I decided to call Mrs. Moffett. I was sitting at the kitchen table and trying to make the call when I heard a noise behind me. First there was a flash of light, and then the room went black.

A terrible pain in the back of my head awoke me. I reached to where the pain was. My hair was crusty. How odd. Why would it be crusty? Blood. It must be blood. I opened my eyes, and I was dizzy. Still, I could manage to see that I was home. But it was dark. What day was it? What time was it?

Grandma. I had to call Grandma. But what was her number? I couldn't remember her number. If it weren't for the pain in my head, I could remember Grandma's number. After all, it had been my number, too, when I lived with her.

"One," a voice said to me. "The number is one."

How could Grandma's number be one? That was too short for a phone number. Nobody's phone number was one. And then I remembered, Grandma's number was in my phone's memory. I looked at the keypad. All I had to do was to press the auto key and then one.

One. Grandma's number was one. I picked up the phone, which was off the hook. I had fallen over right in front of it. How convenient. I nearly giggled for joy, except the pain in my head made it impossible. I depressed the switch hook. A dial tone. The phone still worked. Oh, Jesus, thank you. I pressed auto. Then I pressed one. The phone was ringing.

"Hello." It was Grandmas voice.

"Grandma."

"Carmen, where are you? They just called me a

few minutes ago and said you didn't show up for work."

"Grandma, I'm here. I'm at home. I'm hurt."

"Hurt? My God, what's wrong, Carmen?"

"Somebody hurt me, Grandma. I don't know."

"Carmen, Carmen." She was shouting, but her voice sounded farther and farther away. I couldn't stay awake anymore.

CHAPTER 9

I woke up again, only this time, I was in a white room. I looked up, and there was Grandma, sitting by me.

"Grandma?"

"Carmen, oh, Carmen." She was crying.

"What's wrong? Where am I?" I said.

"St. Joseph's."

"The hospital? What happened to me?"

Grandma shook her head and cried louder. I reached up to feel the back of my head. There was a bandage on it. Grandma was standing by the bed and pressing a button. Soon, a nurse came in.

Then the nurse left, and soon another woman in a lab coat came in. Her name tag said *Dr. Miller*. She asked Grandma to leave.

"Carmen, I'm Doris Miller. I'm a doctor. I'm here to help you."

"I know you're a doctor. It says so on your coat."

"Good," she said.

"Grandma says I'm in the hospital."

"That's right. Do you know what hospital you're in?"

"She told me I'm in St. Joseph's."

"That's right. Do you know what city you're in?"

I thought a while. What city am I in? Of course, I knew that. "Frontier City. I was born here."

"That's right. Do you know who the president is?"

"Ronald Reagan. But I hate him."

"How about that governor?"

The governor. "Mr. Nigh?"

"That's right," Dr. Miller said.

"Why are you asking me these questions?"

"Because, Carmen, I'm a neurologist. I was called in because you got a nasty bump on the head."

"A brain doctor?"

"That's right, Carmen. A brain doctor."

"That's funny. You're a brain doctor."

"Carmen, do you remember what day it is?"

I thought about that one. What day was it? Monday, Tuesday, Wednesday, Thursday, Friday, Saturday, Sunday.

"It must be my day off, because I'm not at work."

"What are your days off?"

"Sunday and Monday."

"It's Tuesday, Carmen."

I tried to sit up, but couldn't.

"What are you doing?"

"I should be at work. My boss will be furious."

"They know you're here. We took care of that. And your father. He's called several times to check on you."

"Where's Julia?"

"Who's Julia?"

"My girlfriend. Julia Nichols. She's an FCU student. I want to see her. Can somebody tell her I'm here?"

"Maybe your grandmother can notify her."

"Grandma doesn't like Julia because we're lesbians."

The doctor showed no reaction. "I see. Well, then I'll see to it that one of the nurses calls her. Do you have her number?"

"She should be at the library right now. The *Frontier City Times* library. You can call her there. Or she's at home. She's in the phone book under J. Nichols. N-I-C-H-O-L-S. I can't think of her number right now for some reason. Isn't that funny?"

"It's not unusual with head injuries. I'll have the nurse get in touch." She bent down and looked at me with concern. "Listen, Carmen, some policemen want to talk with you about how your head got bumped. Do you want to talk to them now?"

"Okay."

Two policemen in street clothes came in. They introduced themselves as Detective David Roberts and Detective Joe Donaldson.

"Do you know why you're here?" Roberts said.

"Yes. I have a nasty bump on the head."

"Do you remember who did it?"

I tried to think. There was nothing. "No."

"Your grandmother said you told her over the phone that somebody had hurt you. Do you remember saying that?"

I made another effort to recall. "No."

"Who is Rachel?"

I knew a Rachel. "Rachel Metcalf? What about her?"

In the ambulance, on the way here, you woke up for a moment and said, "Rachel is in danger. I have to help her," Roberts said.

I tried hard to think. Rachel wasn't in danger. I'd gotten her out of LTU. It must have been a flashback. "I don't remember. I really can't. Not right now."

"Carmen, somebody broke into your apartment, klonked you over the head, and ransacked the place. They left behind a note on your table. Does this look familiar?"

The detective handed me a sheet of paper in a plastic bag with a simple typed message: BUTT OUT OR NEXT TIME YOU DIE.

"I guess I should be afraid."

"We're keeping a uniformed officer at your room round-the-clock. I wouldn't worry. What does the message mean?"

"Listen, my head really hurts, and I need some sleep. Can we talk about this later?"

"The more we talk now, the more chance we have to go out and catch whoever did this to you."

"I know. I know, I said. But there's nothing in my mind right now." I slipped into oblivion.

*　*　*　*　*

I woke up at six. I was clear-headed and my bump didn't hurt nearly as much. Grandma was still sitting by the bed, asleep in her chair. I was grateful to have her there.

She woke up when the nurse came in to take my blood pressure and temperature. "How are you, little one?" Grandma said.

"Fine. I don't remember much about last night. But I do feel better. Where are my cats?"

"Still at your house. I made sure they were locked in. They were okay. They had plenty of food."

At nine, Dr. Miller came around and examined me. She said I could go home that day, provided I stayed with someone who could look after me. That meant staying in Grandma's house. She also advised me to rest a few days before returning to work, keep the wound site dry and clean, and to come back and see her in a week.

When we got home, I headed to the bathroom to inspect the damage. The left side of my face was swollen. With a hand mirror and the bathroom mirror, I inspected the crash site. A white butterfly bandage covered a bald patch that had been shaved on the back of my head. My hair was a greasy mat.

First things first. I decided to shower. Grandma's shampoo smelled like something you would use on a dog, but I gritted my teeth.

Showering proved easy, except for my head. I used a minimum of shampoo, but still my wound stung. Afterwards, I gently toweled off, disinfected the wound, and got dressed.

"Grandma, can you put a new bandage on me?"

She was horrified. "What are you doing getting your head wet, you durn fool?"

"My hair was greasy. I had to wash it."

"Pride goeth before destruction, and a haughty spirit before a fall."

"Create in me a clean hairdo, O God, and renew a right hairdo within me."

She shook a finger under my nose. "Don't you blaspheme the Word of God."

"Forget it. I'll do the bandage."

"No you won't, you durn reprobate." With much grumbling, she put on the bandage.

I picked up the phone and headed to the sofa.

"What do you think you're doing?"

"I have to make some calls."

"You're supposed to rest."

"Grandma, please don't treat me like I'm five years old. I have to make some calls."

"Well, don't get yourself all stirred up," she ordered, and stomped out of the room.

I called my answering machine to retrieve my messages. Julia had called twice, and there was a call from Rachel: "Please help me. The end is near."

Suddenly, my memory was jarred. Rachel had called me just before things had gone black. What was it she had said? "Dirty secrets leave dirty handprints."

I called Julia.

"I tried to come see you," Julia said, "but your grandmother and that cop were standing guard over you like a pair of pit bulls. No way I could get in."

"I'm sure. Listen, I gotta get out of here. It's a

matter of life and death. Rachel called twice. I think she's going to do herself in. She called last night right before I got knocked out. I have to find her."

"Carmen, why don't you leave this stuff to the police? Aren't you already injured enough?"

"I'll call Mrs. Moffett to see whether she's heard something. But I have to get back to my apartment and wait for Rachel to call. I need you to run interference for me and help get me out of here."

"I'll be right over."

I phoned up directory assistance and got Jeannie Moffett's number.

"This is Carla Sullivan —"

"Stop using that name," she said, sounding more worried than wrathful. "The deputy told me you had some Spanish name."

"All right. My name is Carmen Ramirez. I work for the *Frontier City Times.*"

"I knew you were up to something."

"Mrs. Moffett, your granddaughter called me last night. She's in a motel somewhere, and I think she may intend to kill herself."

"Where is she?" she demanded.

"I don't know. That's why I'm calling you. She was trying to tell me something important over the phone. I need to speak to her."

"If you're so concerned about her, why did you wait till now to call me?"

"Mrs. Moffett, I am not the cause of your family's problems. Yesterday afternoon, as I was trying to call you, somebody broke into my house and knocked me out. I was unconscious for several hours. I just got out of the hospital."

She paused. "I'm sorry."

"For some reason, your granddaughter trusts me and wants to tell me something. I think it might give her some peace if she did. Do you have a clue where she might be?"

"No. The sheriff's men are out looking for her now."

"Can you tell me anything that would help? She told me something about dirty secrets and dirty handprints. Do you know what she means?"

"She sounds just like her mama. You figured it out, you know."

"Figured out what?"

"My daughter killed herself, she said stoically. She went off with that man, that Metcalf. Had to have him. Wouldn't wait. Couldn't be talked out of it. Married at nineteen. Dead by her own hand at twenty-five. OD'd on pills. We managed to keep it out of the papers, till you dug it up. I never knew what went wrong with her."

"I am sorry," I said.

"Sorry doesn't do anything."

"I know," I said. "Does Rachel know how her mother died?"

"No. We kept it from both the girls."

"I see," I said. Perhaps she had discovered the truth about her mother's death.

"You find Rachel, now, if you can."

"I'll do my best, Mrs. Moffett."

Within a half-hour, Julia showed up with a bouquet of daisies. Grandma opened the door but wouldn't speak to her.

"Hi, Julia," I said. "Long time no see."

Julia nodded at me nervously as she handed my grandmother the flowers. "Here. These are for you, Mrs. Sullivan."

Grandma glared, first at me, then at Julia. Then she snatched the flowers out of Julia's hand and stomped into the kitchen. I followed her. She was bent over the trash can.

"What are you doing?"

"Throwing these flowers out. They're full of bugs."

I went to the trash to retrieve them. She had torn them to shreds.

I pulled them out. "Why would you do this?"

"I told you — they're full of bugs."

"Grandma, you know that's not true."

"You calling me a liar, girl?"

"I'm leaving," I said.

"I should have known."

"Grandma, Julia is important to me. Can't you even be civil to her?"

"What for? She's your friend, not mine."

"I have things I have to take care of, and I can't do them here. Please understand."

She turned her body away from me. "I know what it is you have to take care of. And it's anything and anybody in the world but me, the grandma who raised you. If you get yourself killed, it's no fault of mine."

It was only a mile from Grandma's house to mine, but I felt weak all the way home, even with

Julia's help. By the time we reached my apartment about a half-hour later, my head was aching and I was queasy.

I was surprised by the scene there. My place was cheerful, clean, and flooded with flowers. Only a boarded-up window reminded me of the break-in the previous day. The cats greeted me at the door.

"Where's all the mess?" I said.

"Mr. Braun took care of the window. And I took care of the blood and gore and mess. Geez, Carmen, that big melon on your neck bled a lot."

"Thanks a lot," I said. "By the way, are you going to stay around to baby-sit me?"

"Of course," she said. "You have nothing to fear."

I checked out the bouquets — they were from Julia, Raúl, Sargent, and Gruber. The cats were having a field day tearing off petals and leaves. I called up Sargent at home to fill him in on my injuries.

"Oh, don't worry about coming back this week," he said. "Just take the rest of the week off. I want you in top form when you come back."

Sargent was being nice? It seemed so out of character. I guess he wasn't all bastard.

"Did you speak to Blazer?"

"Yes. He claims your story is sheer fabrication. I took it up with Ned Foxworth."

The editor in chief of the *Times*. "What did he say?"

"The series is on hold, pending your return to work. We have to see your evidence. I have to tell you — Ron isn't happy about it."

"Thanks for the warning."

"Carmen, lay low for now, and we'll talk later."

That afternoon, the detectives came back to question me. By this time, they'd figured out that I had called the cops before, about the threatening call. They had questioned the neighbors and come up empty. No one had seen anything suspicious. At my request, they questioned Buddy Jefferson, who had alibis for all of Tuesday. He had been at the school working during the day and at Temptations strip bar during the evening with several of his pals. The detectives promised to keep me informed and to have a patrol car keep an eye on the house.

By Thursday afternoon, I had heard nothing from Rachel or Mrs. Moffett. Then, at three o'clock, the phone rang. There was only breathing at the other end.

"Who's there?" I said.

"Carmen? It's Rachel."

"Rachel, thank God you're alive. Where are you?"

"Frontier City."

"Where?"

"Where have you been, Carmen? I needed you."

"I was hurt. I had to go to the hospital Tuesday night. But I'm better. I'm here now. Where are you?"

"I need to talk to you."

"Tell me where you are, and I'll come."

"You have to promise not to bring anyone."

"I promise."

"I'm at the Economy Inn, on the far East Side, right off I-Forty-Four. Room two-forty."

"I'll be there as soon as possible."

Julia was furious. "You are supposed to be resting."

"I have to find out what Rachel's trying to tell me."

"You are recovering from a concussion. You're not going unless you take me with you," she said.

"I can't argue with that," I said.

Twenty minutes later, I saw the orange roof of the Economy Inn, an inexpensive, well-worn motel frequented by truckers and cost-conscious tourists.

"You'd better wait in the car," I said to Julia. "She told me not to bring anyone."

"Fine," Julia said.

"Rachel, it's me, Carmen," I said, knocking on her door. No answer. I was about to fetch the desk clerk when Rachel finally answered my knock. She looked grim and disheveled, her auburn hair matted and her jeans and T-shirt rumpled. She smelled like she hadn't bathed for days. She seemed to recognize me only dimly. Her smoky gray eyes were glassy.

"Hi, kiddo, how's it going?"

"Okay," she said numbly.

"You know who I am?"

"Yeah. Carmen."

"That's right. Do you remember why you called me?"

"Yeah."

"Can I come in?"

She guided me into the room. The drapes were drawn, the only source of light the TV, which was playing silently in the corner. She sat on one of the two queen-size beds, and I sat in a chair next to the window.

"What is it? Tell me. What are the dirty secrets?"

"It's hard for me to feel anything." She rocked back and forth on the bed.

"Are you taking anything?"

"Stuff from my psychiatrist."

"Did you take too many?"

"I don't know," she said, her voice devoid of emotion.

"You don't have to tell me unless you want to. Do you want to tell somebody?"

She didn't reply. She stared into space as she kept rocking.

"Is this about your mother's death?"

"What about it?" Rachel said.

She didn't know about the suicide. "Rachel, I don't understand why you called me."

"You got me out of there. I can trust you, right?"

"You can trust me. Tell me what it is."

"Daddy," she whispered.

"You want to tell your father?"

"No," she said emphatically.

"Then what?"

Rachel looked up at me. I could tell that the pills hadn't numbed all of her pain. "Daddy did things. To me and Rebecca. Dirty things."

Oh my God. Incest.

"He started when we were real young. I can't remember a lot of it. It's like I've lost that part of me. I wasn't in my body sometimes, you know?"

I didn't, but I nodded at her.

Rachel clawed at the bedspread as she spoke. "Before she, uh, died, Rebecca told me he was getting her ready for, well, you know — intercourse. He had been using a rubber thing on her, and it hurt. You know. Like a sex toy. He has a whole box of them."

Dear God.

Her voice stayed flat. Her face was numb. Only her angry, clawing hands revealed her pain. "He called us his little wives. Just like Lot's daughters, he always said. He would get what he wanted. He could be mean or he could be nice. But Daddy always got his way."

I was overcome with horror, but I struggled to keep my face neutral.

"The night before she died, Rebecca told me she was going to get help. She told me she was going to her teacher's house. She had found Miss Barrett's address when she was in the principal's office. She'd been sent there for punishment, you know. She was in trouble a lot. Rebecca sneaked into the desk while the principal was out of the room. She was a brave little girl." Tears began rolling down Rachel's face.

"She came home from school that day. Daddy took her into his — his bedroom. She gritted her teeth. I knew what he was doing to her. I couldn't stop him."

She sighed. Her rocking grew more frantic. "Then, she went off for her music lesson. Only she didn't show up. The music teacher called. So Daddy came to ask where Rebecca was."

"You don't know what it was like," she said, gasping for breath now. "He got rough. I resisted for as long as I could. But he could be so cruel. He pinched me. All over, you know. All over." She slammed the bed with her hand.

191

"He made me talk. I told him she'd gone to Miss Barrett's house. He followed her there. When he came back, he told me Rebecca was dead and I would be too if I ever told anybody what had happened. I believed him."

The pain and shame of years of torture flooded in on her. She collapsed on the bed and sobbed uncontrollably.

Numbly, I made a suggestion. "Rachel, I think you need to go to the hospital."

"You don't believe me," she said.

"Yes I do. But I also know that you're very sick right now, and I don't think you can take care of yourself. Abuse like that leaves deep scars. I think you need to go."

Rachel said, "Just don't take me to Vinewood."

"Why not?"

"I hated it. Too many drugs. I felt dead there."

"Okay," I said.

Julia and I took Rachel to Frontier City Psychiatric Center and checked her in. I called her grandmother from the hospital.

"You found her?" Mrs. Moffett said.

"Yes. I've taken her to the psych center here in Frontier City. She was at the Economy Inn."

"How is she?"

"She's in rough shape mentally. I think you need to get up here and make sure her father is kept away from her."

"Why?"

"Rachel says a lot of abuse went on."

192

"What kind of abuse?"

"Brace yourself. Extreme sexual abuse. Of both girls."

"Sexual abuse?"

"That's what Rachel told me."

"I don't believe it," she said, her voice stunned and flat.

"That's what she said, Mrs. Moffett. Anyway, who was responsible for putting her in Vinewood?"

"Her father."

"She insisted she didn't want to go back there. So make sure she doesn't go back there. All right?"

"Yes, of course."

"Who is her psychiatrist?"

"Dr. Nelson Phillips, head of psychiatry out there."

"I see," I said. "Well, she's safe now. I have some other things to take care of."

"Thanks for finding her, Carmen."

As soon, as I hung up, I called Vinewood Hospital and asked for the P.R. department. I spoke to a very bubbly woman named Sandy.

"Who is the head of your psychiatry department?"

"Dr. Nelson Phillips," said Sandy.

"And where did he earn his medical degree?" I asked.

"Just a sec. I'll have to look that up."

Moments later, Sandy returned with the information: "Dr. Nelson Phillips was a graduate of Lovell Taft University Medical School."

On the way back to my apartment, Julia and I discussed the case.

"Her psychiatrist is an LTU grad, and I suspect he may be a buddy of the Reverend. I think he's been keeping her quiet — with drugs — since the murder," I said.

"You might be overdramatizing things, Carmen."

"I don't think so. Metcalf seems to be loaded with cash. The Sunday I went to his church, the bulletin said they took in over thirty-five thousand bucks in a week. I think he has enough money to buy off anybody he wants."

"But that's the church's money. Not his."

"With a large cash offering, anything is possible. Anyway, I think we should go to the cops with the information we have."

"Now there's where I agree with you."

When we got into the house, the phone was ringing.

The voice was male, guttural, menacing: "We have your grandmother. Meet us on the west side of the old rail depot parking lot in half an hour if you ever want to see her alive again. Don't even think about contacting the police. She'll be dead before they arrive."

"Holy shit," I said. I immediately called my grandmother's house. No answer.

"Shit," I said. "She's not there."

"Carmen, we have to call the police. It's obviously a trap."

"No."

"You're being irrational."

"I'm leaving." I headed for the door.

"Hold on," Julia said. "I'm coming with you."

We arrived at my grandmother's house. Her LTD was in the driveway, and everything looked normal, until we got to the back door. It was hanging open.

I ran into the house. "Grandma!" I shouted. It was empty. She was gone.

"I guess we're going to have to play it their way," I said as I stood in her empty living room.

I looked at the mantel over her false fireplace. There were pictures on it: of me as a baby in the lap of my red-headed mother; my grandfather, smoking his pipe, in his recliner; Uncle Buster with a stringer of fish; Buster and my mother, as teens, playing a duet at the family piano. I looked away.

"Julia, what am I going to do?"

"Can you take me by the dorm? I need to pick something up."

"Now?" I said frantically.

"Now." Julia was emphatic.

We headed over to Smith Hall. I must have been doing at least fifty in a thirty-mile-an-hour zone, but I didn't care.

I stopped out front while Julia ran in. She was back in under two minutes. She was carrying a long cloth case.

"What's that — a pool cue?" I said, bewildered.

"I'm armed," she said. She opened the case. It contained a very long gun.

"What the hell is that?" I said, aghast.

"My grandfather's hunting rifle. My dad gave it to me for graduation."

"Can you use it?"

"I'm from Arkansas. Pistols. Shotguns. Rifles. Crossbows. You name it. I shoot it."

"Ever hit anything?"

"Targets. Skeet. Bleach bottles. Watermelons."

"We'll have to hope we're attacked by giant watermelons."

We headed out to the abandoned depot — Julia, I, and the big, long gun. It was too bad Clint Eastwood wasn't with us.

We had a plan. Not a sophisticated plan, but a plan. I was to drop Julia off before I got to the parking lot. She was to follow from a distance. As soon as I gave her the signal that I knew where Grandma was, she was to come in, gun blazing, if necessary, and screaming that the cops were on the way. It was the sort of thing that would only work in a movie staring Charles Bronson.

I dropped her off in a wooded area near the abandoned depot.

"You know where we are?"

"Sure, Carmen. Don't worry about me. I know how to take care of myself in the woods."

"Okay, kiddo. I just want to say, if I don't come out of this alive, I love you. And if you can't save us, save yourself."

"I love you too."

We kissed quickly. She jumped out of the car, and off I went.

With my motor idling, I waited. My heart was filled with thoughts of Julia: her love for me, her courage, her willingness to put her life on the line for me and for Grandma. There were so many things I wanted to tell her. And then I thought of my grandma, the only mother I had ever known. A stubborn, hateful, overbearing woman whom I loved more than my own life. "Please, God," I whispered, "bring us out of this alive."

Just then, a black Lincoln Continental rolled up next to the Honda. The window came down. It was Metcalf at the wheel, and Blazer with him. Grandma was nowhere to be seen.

"Get in," Metcalf said.

What the hell was going on? Blazer and Metcalf? Then, it dawned on me that the message said, "We have your grandmother."

"Where is she?"

"Safe and sound," Metcalf said in a shaky voice. His eyes were nervous and uncertain. His pompadour was disheveled.

"If I get in that car, you're going to take me out somewhere and kill me. Now you turn my grandmother loose."

"Nobody's going to hurt you, or your grandmother," Metcalf said.

"Of course not," Blazer said. "We just have a small matter to settle."

"What do you want, Blazer?"

"The letters I wrote to Diane."

"I don't have them."

"I know that."

So they must have been responsible for knocking me out and ransacking my apartment.

"Where are they?" he demanded.

"Somewhere where you'll never reach them," I

said, hoping Ruby had put them in the safe-deposit box.

"Carmen, we're going to get that information out of you one way or another," Blazer said. "We do have your grandmother."

"You can't get away with this. Too many people know. You're forgetting Rachel. She's still alive, and she's ready to talk about the abuse," I said.

"What did she tell you?" Metcalf said, panicked.

"Everything. Even about your box of sex toys. And if she told me, she'll tell others. Like the police."

"Calm down, Rev. That's easy enough to take care of," Blazer said.

"She's in the hospital. And not Vinewood either. You can't reach her."

"With the Reverend here and his money, we can always reach her. There's always an underpaid orderly who can be bribed. Thanks for the information," Blazer said.

Blazer turned to the Reverend. "Go get her out of the goddamned car, pastor."

Metcalf nodded at him. I heard the car door open. I shoved the stick shift into first and gunned across the parking lot, away from the Lincoln. Spinning the Honda around, I built up speed as I headed straight at their car. Metcalf finally got the hint, jumped back into the car, and started to back away. I managed to ram into the front of the Lincoln with all the little Honda had to give. The crash was huge and deafening. The kamikaze spirit lived on in my little Japanese car.

I shoved open the door and took off into the woods. I heard metal creaking and groaning as

Metcalf attempted to move his car. I hoped I had disabled it.

Crouching behind some bushes and breathing heavily, I watched the parking lot. Blazer got out on the passenger side and ran into the woods, away from my hiding place. Why was he running? Was he looking for me? Was he going to hurt Grandma?

"Ron, come back here," Metcalf shouted, getting out of the car. For a while, he simply stood there. Then he shouted: "Carmen, I still have your grandmother." He walked to the trunk and opened it. She's back here. "I think you killed her."

Just then, a shot rang out, and Metcalf crumpled.

Fearing the worst, I bolted out of the bushes toward the car. Metcalf was writhing on the ground. His shirt was drenched with blood. He'd been hit in the shoulder. Beside him was a shotgun.

Julia came trotting out of the woods. "Get that gun away from him," she warned. "Don't move," she ordered Metcalf as she trained the rifle at his skull.

I nodded at her and picked up the gun. I bent over him.

"Now, you filthy son of a bitch, where is my grandmother?"

He moaned but did not answer me.

I poked his wound with the barrel of the shotgun.

Metcalf shouted in pain. "Back seat of the car."

"Watch him, Julia."

I opened the back door, and there, facedown on the floor was my grandmother trussed up with duct tape. She was moaning and struggling furiously against her bonds. She was okay.

"She's alive," I shouted to Julia. "She's tied up. I

don't think I can get her out of here. I'll need a knife."

"Carmen," Julia said. "Get on his CB and get the cops out here. He's losing a lot of blood. Channel Nine."

"Grandma, we'll have you out of here in a minute," I assured her.

As sirens approached, I heard a noise coming out of Metcalf, so I bent over him. He was crying. He must have thought he was dying. I decided to encourage the thought.

"You've lost a lot of blood, Metcalf. You might not make it."

"I don't want to burn in hell." His face was white with panic.

"You have something you want to get off your conscience?"

"I didn't mean to kill her. I just wanted her to come back home. She kept defying me. I hit her harder than I meant to. She hit the table. And then, there was all that blood. Blazer showed up right after it happened. I don't know where he came from. Maybe the devil sent him. He said he would help me. He told me what to do."

"He told me to wipe off every place I'd touched. He said he'd take care of getting rid of the diary. Rebecca brought it with her, to show her teacher. She'd written down everything I'd done to her. Only he never got rid of the diary."

Metcalf, his face twisted with pain, gulped air. "He's been blackmailing me for years. Hundreds of thousands of dollars. I paid him off as a consultant to my ministry. He set up the teacher to take the fall for me. He convinced her she'd never be able to prove her innocence — because of the drinking and the homosexuality. And then he wrote those stories in the newspaper. I didn't know she was going to take her own life. Blazer hated her, wanted to ruin her. That can't be my fault, can it?"

I said nothing.

He looked at me beseechingly. "You understand, don't you? I have so much blood on my hands. Rebecca was my daughter. I didn't want her to die. Lord Jesus, please forgive me."

He was pathetic. For a moment, I almost felt sorry for him.

Within minutes, we were surrounded by a dozen black-and-whites.

First thing, the cops seized Julia's gun as well as the gun I held. I quickly told them about Blazer's escape.

"Is he armed?" a cop asked.

I didn't think the master manipulator had a taste for violence. "I don't know," I told the cop. "But you'd better check in on Ruby Weller. He might well be after her."

He agreed to radio a patrol car to check on her. As he walked away, I flagged down another cop.

"My grandmother," I said. "She's in the back seat."

"Stay here," he ordered.

"She's been through hell. I want to be with her," I said.

The cop cut Grandma loose from her bonds. The last to come off was her gag.

I helped her sit up in the back seat. I noticed that her mouth was covered with blood. "Did they hit you? Are you hurt, Grandma?"

She finally spoke: "I bit one of those sons of bitches when he tried to put the gag on me. I kicked the other one in the balls."

When the ambulances got there, Grandma refused to go, but I insisted.

She had a few bumps and bruises and a cracked rib from her ordeal, but other than that, she was fine. I had a slightly banged-up knee and elbow that didn't even hurt until the next day. Metcalf had a shattered shoulder and a large bite wound on his hand. He would live — to go to prison, I hoped.

CHAPTER 10

Over the next few weeks, I was pulled off the copy desk to work with Jeff Green on the Metcalf case. Green was nice enough and pragmatic enough to realize he couldn't behave otherwise. His police contacts made it much easier to collect information. So, sharing a byline with him didn't bother me. The truth was coming out. At least some of it.

After his release from Frontier General Hospital, Metcalf was transferred to Frontier County Jail, where he was held on charges of murder, kidnapping, conspiracy to kidnap, assault, battery, incest, child abuse, and grand theft. Police found evidence that Metcalf had been skimming church and university funds to the tune of a couple of million dollars. Investigators were tracing bank records to prove that he had been using at least some of that money to pay Nelson Phillips, his old college buddy, to keep Rachel drugged, crazy, and quiet. He had also paid Blazer half a million dollars as a public relations consultant to his ministry. After hiring the best criminal law firm in the state, he pleaded not guilty to all the charges — by reason of insanity.

The D.A.s office assigned an ace prosecutor — Gloria Ford, a young, ambitious, bright assistant D.A. — to the case.

Early in the morning the day after Blazer's escape, the cops had found the fugitive near the Texas border. He had limped back to his car — thanks to Grandma's well-placed kick — and headed south. Bryan County sheriff's deputies caught him on a two-lane back road fifteen miles from the Red River. He was transferred to the Frontier County Jail, where he was held on charges of accessory to murder, obstruction of justice, extortion, kidnapping, and assault. He pleaded not guilty to all charges, but rumor had it that the D.A.'s office would not seek a life term if Blazer would turn state's evidence on the murder charges.

The last thing anyone knew about Phillips was that he was headed to Rio de Janeiro. When and if he ever returned, he would face a criminal trial and hearings before the hospital board and the county medical board on his treatment of Rachel, whom, over the years, he had doped nearly into oblivion.

School superintendent Richard Farmer announced school board hearings aimed at clearing any roadblocks preventing school staffers from reporting the suspected sexual abuse of students. Ruby and her fellow teachers weren't willing to go on the record to complain about Dr. Hawkins' failure to press for a psychological evaluation of Rebecca, and she couldn't be held accountable for Buddy's prison record. School personnel were hired by the district, not the principal, so Hawkins would retain her post.

Buddy was immediately suspended from working at the school. After he lost his job, he started calling me up and threatening my life. I reported the calls to the police, and this time, they were not only willing to listen, they monitored the line. Buddy was charged with making terroristic threats. Released on bond, he had jumped bail and was being sought by the authorities.

In a smaller matter, my complaint against Deputy Clyde Davis resulted in a letter of apology. He asked my forgiveness for slurring on Spanish people. I had to smile.

In the newsroom, my phone rang.

"*Times,* Carmen Ramirez."

"Hello," said the voice. "This is Lovell Taft. The sound was unmistakably his — commanding, urgent, yet gentle."

"Reverend Taft," I said, "thanks for returning my call."

"What can I do for you?"

"I have a few questions about the Metcalf case. What do you think about the charges against Bobby Ray?"

"No comment."

"What about the allegations that he skimmed university funds?"

"I have nothing to say about that, young lady."

"What about you? Didn't Metcalf hurt you as well? By entering an insanity plea, he is, in effect, admitting that he committed the crimes. You have frequently referred to him as being like a son to you. How does this make you feel?"

"Carmen, I am shepherd to a large flock. I can't be a stumbling block to others. I have to be strong and lay my concerns at the foot of the cross. We don't always understand what happens in this life. We just have to trust in Jesus for the strength to bear up under it," he said, his voice cracking.

"Why have you visited him several times since his arrest? My sources at the jail tell me you've been there four or five times."

"My purpose there is pastoral."

"I see," I said. "Have you forgiven him?"

"The Bible says, 'If thy brother offend thee, rebuke him; and if he repent, forgive him.' "

"And what about what he did to Rachel and Rebecca? Is that forgivable?"

"I'm going to share a little wisdom with you. Jesus says in Matthew 18: 'Whosoever shall offend one of these little ones who believe in me, it were better for him that a millstone were hanged about his neck and that he were drowned in the depth of the sea.' "

I found myself spellbound by his voice.

He continued: "This is just between you and me. Rachel can have anything she needs. She'll never go without. She can come back to this university or go elsewhere. And remember this, Carmen: We serve a mighty God. He can heal the broken mind and the shattered heart."

I paused, unable to reply. Taft had me reeling with emotion — the same feeling I had had at twelve, when I walked up in front of all my fellow campers to get saved at church camp.

"Carmen, you were an instrument of God's judgment in all this. The Bible says: 'For there is nothing covered that shall not be revealed; neither hidden, that shall not be known. Therefore, whatever ye have spoken in darkness shall be heard in the light; and that which ye have spoken in the ear in closets shall be proclaimed upon the housetops.'"

Chosen by God to proclaim the sins of others from the housetops. It was a tough position to be in. I didn't know what to say.

"Do you have any comment about Blazer's role in all this?"

"I simply will not comment on this case. It's a matter for God and the criminal justice system to sort out."

"I guess that's all then, Reverend, and thanks for calling me back."

"I'll be praying for you, Carmen. The Lord has a plan for every life. Keep that in mind."

Rachel greeted me with a tentative smile as she walked into the visitors lounge at Frontier City

Psychiatric Center. She looked frail and thin as she sat across from me in her jeans and a faded blue sweat shirt.

"How are you doing?" I asked her.

"It's hard," she said. Her face was full of pain, but she looked alive again. "They don't have me on a lot of medication. I can finally think and feel and remember. The nightmares come almost all the time. It hurts. It hurts all the time."

Her pain was beyond my comprehension. I didn't pretend to understand it. "When do you go home?"

"My doctor wants me to leave as soon as possible. I think I'll feel stronger soon."

"I hope so. You know, Rachel, a lot of people have been through what you have. I think you'll find a lot of strength and support if you talk to them."

She nodded, sweeping her auburn hair away from her eyes. "That's what my doctor says. I've spent some time already in group therapy here."

"Listen, if you ever feel like talking, call me."

She nodded again without looking at me.

I was nearly out the door when she called: "Carmen, wait a minute."

"Yes," I said.

"Listen, would it help your career if I gave you an interview?"

"Rachel, if you ever want to tell your story to the public, just let me know. I'd be glad to write it up. But I'll only do it if you want to tell the story. Don't do it for me."

"Thanks. For everything." She smiled bravely at me.

On my way out, I ran into Mrs. Moffett. She

looked tired and shaken in her worn floral dress and straw hat. "Hello there," she said to me.

"How are you, ma'am?"

"I'll live," she said. "I want to thank you for all you did for Rachel. She's hurting, but the doctors say that's part of the recovery."

"I'm sure it must be hard to watch."

"I also want to apologize for my rudeness."

"I understand. You were trying to protect your family."

"I didn't do a very good job at that," she said. "My daughter OD'd on pills. My granddaughters were molested by their own daddy. One's dead. I didn't do a very good job."

"It's not your fault. Metcalf is a brilliant con man. He conned a whole church. He conned Lovell Taft. How could you know?"

"That may be true, but I still feel bad about it." She twisted a handkerchief she was holding.

"Rachel needs you now. I think you can help each other."

We shook hands and I left.

It was a Saturday night — my first night back on the copy desk. Near the end of the shift, Sargent offered drinks at Bailey's.

"Carmen," he called to me, "be there."

"I really have to get home."

"Stop backing out, you little snob. And that's an order."

So I sat at the table between Sargent and

Gruber as the cocktail waitress, a woman in her early twenties with a microscopically short skirt and jet-black dyed hair, took orders from the copy desk crowd. I was the only woman in the bunch. The bar was old and dingy, and a no-frills place for hard drinkers.

I ordered a ginger ale, and Sargent gave me a disapproving look.

"Ralph, I'm driving," I said.

"I'll call you a taxi," Sargent said.

"I don't want to drink tonight, Ralph."

"I'll take you home if you want to get plastered," Gruber offered.

"No thanks, fellows. My order stands."

After taking off his coat and tie so he could get down to some serious drinking, Sargent ordered a double scotch, neat, and downed it quickly. Gruber got a Bud Light and started mooning at me with his big brown eyes. I turned my chair away and tried to ignore him.

"Listen, Carmen," Sargent said, "let's go to another table. I want to have a word with you in private." I followed him to a corner booth.

"I brought you here for a reason," he said. "I have to talk to you, and I wanted to get you out of the newsroom to do it."

"Sure. What's up?"

"It's no secret that you did a very gutsy thing, and you saved the paper a lot of embarrassment. And you cleared that woman's name."

"Thanks, Ralph."

"Anyway, I had to go all the way to the publisher for this, but you're getting a bonus and a raise. Don't think I'm going to go easy on you

210

because of all this. You still need to work on your headlines, Carmen. They need more punch."

Just then, Gruber walked over with a fresh beer. "Hey, come back, you two. You're spoiling the party. Private powwows are against the rules." His speech was already a little slurred. The Missouri boy couldn't hold his beer. He slid into the booth and draped his arm around me. I pulled away, as far as I could.

"Gruber, get lost. We came over here to have a private conversation," Sargent said. "And stop drooling on the lady."

Gruber retreated sheepishly.

"Jesus H. Christ, what a asshole. No wonder he can't get laid," Sargent said. "How's your head?"

"It doesn't hurt much anymore. There's just a little knot back there. I don't think there'll be any permanent damage."

"What about the car? Can it be fixed?"

"It's a total loss. I don't think the insurance company is going to pay for it because I deliberately wrecked it."

"Listen, I'm going back to the publisher. I'll see what we can do about covering whatever expenses you can't recover. I'll also check into getting you some legal help in dealing with the insurance company."

"I don't know what to say."

"Don't say anything then. And remember what I said about those headlines." The old Marine winked at me.

"I'll work on it."

* * * * *

That Monday, I deposited the bonus and sent Raúl a check to pay back his loan. He'd called several times, and I'd filled him in on the entire story. Well, almost. Julia would be the next chapter to relate. By the end of the week, I picked up a new Honda Civic. The paper had agreed to take on the insurance company on my behalf.

Sunday afternoon, I was on the phone with Grandma.

"Please," I said.

"No."

"She helped save your life."

"It was not God's will for me to go yet."

"She risked her life for you."

"That's fine. She's ruining yours."

"Can't you just come for a little while? Just have some tea or coffee and then leave if you're uncomfortable."

"You know what tea does to my bladder."

"All right. You don't have to come."

Later that day, I was again on the phone.

"I can't wait until you meet her," I said.

"I just hope this one has a sense of humor," Charles said.

"Oh, she's wonderful. You'll love her."

"It's only important that you love her, dear."

"Well, anyway, I'm so glad we'll see you at Christmas. Good luck with the new beau."

"Thanks, darling. I just know it's fate this time. David and I are just meant for each other."

Later, Julia and I sat outside and looked at the stars in the vast Oklahoma sky. For the first time that year, a hint of fall was in the air.

"Have you thought about where you're going to live next semester?" I said.

"The dorm is probably the cheapest way to go."

"What would you think about moving in with me?"

Julia looked at me. "Are you sure you would want me?"

"I think it's something we should consider. You're over here all the time anyway. Why pay double rent when we're spending nearly every night together?"

"My parents would hate it."

"So what? They hate me anyway. And let's not even talk about Louanne."

"What about your grandmother? She'll have a cow or two."

"She'll get over it," I said. "Besides, you're my best friend and I love you."

Julia nodded. "You're my best friend too. And I love you. Do you think we can put up with each other?"

"I don't think that will be a problem."

We sat together contented in the night air.

A few of the publications of
THE NAIAD PRESS, INC.
P.O. Box 10543 • Tallahassee, Florida 32302
Phone (904) 539-5965
Toll-Free Order Number: 1-800-533-1973
Mail orders welcome. Please include 15% postage.

FLASHPOINT by Katherine V. Forrest. 256 pp. Lesbian
blockbuster! ISBN 1-56280-043-4 $22.95

CROSSWORDS by Penny Sumner. 256 pp. 2nd VictoriaCross
Mystery. ISBN 1-56280-064-7 9.95

SWEET CHERRY WINE by Carol Schmidt. 240 pp. A novel of
suspense. ISBN 1-56280-063-9 9.95

CERTAIN SMILES by Dorothy Tell. 224 pp. Erotic short stories
ISBN 1-56280-066-3 9.95

EDITED OUT by Lisa Haddock. 224 pp. 1st Carmen Ramirez
Mystery. ISBN 1-56280-077-9 9.95

WEDNESDAY NIGHTS by Camarin Grae. 288 pp. Sexy
adventure. ISBN 1-56280-060-4 10.95

SMOKEY O by Celia Cohen. 176 pp. Relationships on the playing
field. ISBN 1-56280-057-4 9.95

KATHLEEN O'DONALD by Penny Hayes. 256 pp. Rose and
Kathleen find each other and employment in 1909 NYC.
ISBN 1-56280-070-1 9.95

STAYING HOME by Elisabeth Nonas. 256 pp. Molly and Alix
want a baby . . . or do they? ISBN 1-56280-076-0 10.95

TRUE LOVE by Jennifer Fulton. 240 pp. Six lesbians searching for
love in all the "right" places. ISBN 1-56280-035-3 9.95

GARDENIAS WHERE THERE ARE NONE by Molleen Zanger.
176 pp. Why is Melanie inextricably drawn to the old house?
ISBN 1-56280-056-6 9.95

MICHAELA by Sarah Aldridge. 256 pp. A "Sarah Aldridge"
romance. ISBN 1-56280-055-8 10.95

KEEPING SECRETS by Penny Mickelbury. 208 pp. A Gianna
Maglione Mystery. First in a series. ISBN 1-56280-052-3 9.95

THE ROMANTIC NAIAD edited by Katherine V. Forrest &
Barbara Grier. 336 pp. Love stories by Naiad Press authors.
ISBN 1-56280-054-X 14.95